Have you been invited to all these sleepovers?

The Sleepover Club Best Friends
The Sleepover Club TV Stars
The Sleepover Club Dance-off!
The Sleepover Club Hit the Beach!

Coming soon...

The Sleepover Club Pet Detectives
The Sleepover Club Hey Baby!

The SleePover Club

Dance-Off!

Harriet Castor

HarperCollins *Children's Books*

The Sleepover Club ® is a registered trademark
of HarperCollins*Publishers* Ltd

First published in Great Britain as *Sleepover Girls go Dancing*
by HarperCollins *Children's Books* in 2001
This edition published by HarperCollins *Children's Books* in 2008
HarperCollins *Children's Books* is a division of HarperCollins*Publishers* Ltd,
77-85 Fulham Palace Road, Hammersmith, London W6 8JB

www.harpercollinschildrensbooks.co.uk

1

Text copyright © Harriet Castor 2008

Original series characters, plotlines and settings © Rose Impey 1997

The author asserts the moral right to be
identified as the author of this work.

ISBN-13 978-0-00-726492-6
ISBN-10 0-00-726492-5

Printed and bound in England by
Clays Ltd, St Ives plc

Mixed Sources
Product group from well-managed
forests and other controlled sources
www.fsc.org Cert no. SW-COC-1806
© 1996 Forest Stewardship Council
FSC

FSC is a non-profit international organisation established to promote the
responsible management of the world's forests. Products carrying the FSC
label are independently certified to assure consumers that they come
from forests that are managed to meet the social, economic and
ecological needs of present and future generations.

Find out more about HarperCollins and the environment at
www.harpercollins.co.uk/green

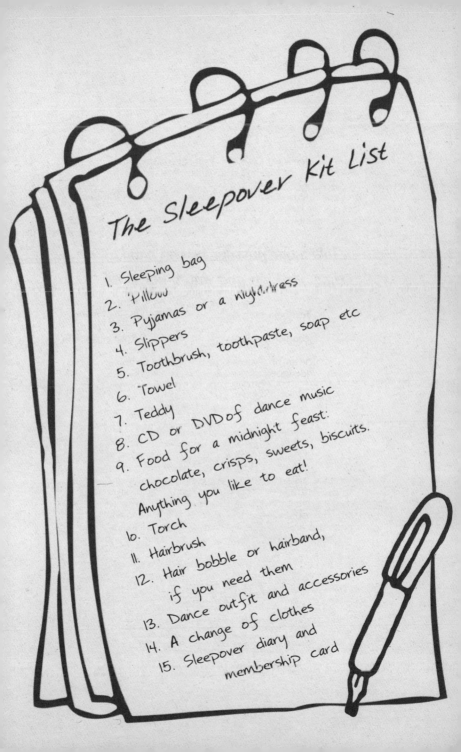

The Sleepover Kit List

1. Sleeping bag
2. Pillow
3. Pyjamas or a nightdress
4. Slippers
5. Toothbrush, toothpaste, soap etc
6. Towel
7. Teddy
8. CD or DVD of dance music
9. Food for a midnight feast: chocolate, crisps, sweets, biscuits. Anything you like to eat!
10. Torch
11. Hairbrush
12. Hair bobble or hairband, if you need them
13. Dance outfit and accessories
14. A change of clothes
15. Sleepover diary and membership card

Take your partner by the hand...
Fling her high and watch her land!

Hey, can I grab you for this one? I've been looking for you everywhere. It's Rosie – remember me? Course you do! Woah, watch out for Kenny! When she gets on the dance floor, you have to keep out of the way – she's like some crazy firework, shooting off in all directions. And just look at Frankie go! She's strutting her stuff like she's on the telly – she could be one of the Sugababes.

Hang on, maybe we should sit out for a

minute, so I can fill you in on all the goss. The last day of term is always a bit crazy, but you won't believe what's happened this time. You'll be on the edge of your seat when I tell you, I guarantee it.

Talking of seats, let's park ourselves on these chairs. We need a quiet corner or Fliss'll hop over and butt in, cos it's such a great story and she reckons she stars in it. I know she's dying to tell you everything, but I found you first!

You remember us all, don't you? The Sleepover Club. There's me, of course, and Fliss – Felicity Sidebotham, if you want to be formal. Poor Fliss – her surname makes the M&Ms snigger, but don't worry, we're always thinking of ways to get back at them for it. The M&Ms – that's Emma Hughes and Emily Berryman (yeuch!) – are our worst enemies at school.

Then there's Frankie. You can never miss her, she's so loud and funny, and dressed up in mad clothes half the time. She'll boss you around too, given the chance! And Kenny – Laura McKenzie to the teachers, but don't call her that or she'll karate-chop you! Kenny's wild. She's football-crazy, for a start, and always coming up with outrageous schemes too. You've got to watch her, especially when the M&Ms are nearby. There's nothing Kenny wouldn't do!

Last but not least there's Lyndz. Look – she's over there, dancing with Frankie. Laughing Lyndz she should be called, cos she's always cheerful and loves giggling. Except with Lyndz, two seconds of giggling turns into hiccups, and that's that!

As the Sleepover Club we have the coolest time staying at each other's houses every week. The Trouble Club, my brother Adam calls us – what a cheek! Except, when you've heard what's just happened to us, I guess you might agree with him...

It all started a few weeks ago, in the middle of a history lesson (yawn!), when Frankie started squealing. Now Frankie's not one to make a fuss about nothing, so when I heard her making that noise –

"*Aieee!*"

– and saw her leap out of her chair as if she had a party popper up her bottom, I thought something major had happened, like the M&Ms had put slimy slugs in her socks.

"Francesca Thomas, whatever is the matter?" said our teacher, Mrs Weaver.

Frankie had her fingers in the back of her collar, and she was jumping up and down as if she was trying to shake something out of her clothes.

"What did you put down her neck?" Kenny yelled at the M&Ms, who had been sitting right behind Frankie.

"Laura, sit down!" barked Mrs Weaver.

"Nothing, *stoo*-pid," smirked Emma 'the Queen' Hughes. "We always knew she had ants in her smelly pants."

I could see Kenny seething at that. The M&Ms are so snooty and babyish, it's just gross. Then I saw it. *Plip*! A big splodge of water landing on Frankie's chair. I looked up.

"Mrs Weaver!" I said, pointing up to the ceiling. "Something's dripping!"

It turned out that the classroom roof had sprung a leak right over Frankie's chair, and it had dripped ice-cold water down the back of her neck. Mrs Weaver cheerfully sent Danny McCloud to get a bucket from the cleaners' cupboard. It was weird. She usually got really narked about stuff like this.

Frankie had to move seats. "What's got into Weaver?" she whispered to me as she went by.

"P'rhaps she's won the lottery," I hissed back.

"She wouldn't be giving us a history lesson if she had," muttered Lyndz, who was sitting next to me. "She'd be in Barbados by now."

Just the mention of Barbados made me go all dreamy – thinking of hot sun, and sandy beaches and palm trees, or whatever they have over there. We used to go on ace holidays abroad when Mum and Dad were still together.

Since they split up and Mum started college, though, we can't afford it, worse luck. So here I was, stuck with my dreams on a wet wintry Wednesday in Cuddington.

But not everyone was feeling grumpy. When the bell was about to go for break Mrs Weaver said, with a big smile on her face, "I have some really exciting news."

"I knew it!" I heard Kenny mutter. "She's got engaged to Prince William!"

Lyndz snorted into her pencil case. I thought she was going to get the giggles, but Mrs Weaver gave her a stern look.

Then Mrs Weaver unrolled a glossy poster and pinned it up on the classroom wall.

Fliss gasped. Kenny groaned. The poster said *British National Ballet* on it, and showed a picture of two dancers in sparkly costumes. The woman was standing on her toes and wearing a tiara. No wonder Fliss was excited. Anything princessy is right up her street.

"Are we going on a trip?" asked Alana 'Banana'

Palmer, one of the M&Ms' geeky friends.

"Better than that," said Mrs Weaver. "The British National Ballet is coming to us! The company's performing in Leicester at the moment, and two of its dancers will be spending the whole day at Cuddington Primary tomorrow, as part of their 'Theatre in Education' project. They'll take each class for a workshop, and then at the end of the afternoon they'll give a demonstration in the school hall."

"But isn't a workshop where you do woodwork and stuff?" asked Danny McCloud.

"Will we have to wear a tutu and pink shoes?" Alana shouted out.

"Yeah, even the boys!" laughed Frankie.

"Now wait a minute," said Mrs Weaver. "Let me explain. This is a *different* sort of workshop, Danny, and no, Alana, there'll be no special clothes required. You'll just need your P.E. kit. It'll be like those 'Music and Movement' lessons we have instead of P.E. on wet days, except that the dancers will be in charge instead of me."

"Well, this is just *awesome*," said Kenny sarcastically, when the bell had finally gone and the five of us were clustered round her desk. It was a wet break, so everyone had to stay in the classroom. Mr Pownall, the other Year 6 teacher, was supervising us. "Just because Weaver likes ballet, why does she have to inflict it on the rest of us? They'll have us prancing around pretending to be fairies, I bet. I wish we were having a couple of Leicester City players to visit instead." (Oh – Kenny is a major fan of Leicester City Football Club. Did I forget to tell you?)

"It'll be excellent!" said Fliss. "I've never seen real live dancers close-up before. I wonder if they'll bring proper costumes with them..." She took the top off Kenny's new silver pen and started doodling, designing some sort of weird ballet outfit.

"You might get to dance with Ryan Scott, Fliss," suggested Frankie in a silky, tempting voice. "He'd make such a good prince, don't you think?" Fliss looked up with a sudden eager expression, and the rest of us cracked up laughing.

"You're all horrible!" she scowled, turning pink and hunching over her drawing again. She was bent so low, her nose was practically touching it.

"Ohmigosh, forget all that. There's something much more exciting!" said Kenny suddenly, smacking herself on the forehead. "I can't believe I haven't told you yet!"

"What, what?" said Lyndz.

"My folks said we can have a sleepover at my place this Friday!"

"Way to go!" Frankie yelled, and we all did high fives and had a group hug. We hadn't had a sleepover for a few weeks and we'd been missing them badly.

"Let's make it a themed one!" I said.

"Yes – ballet!" said Fliss straight away.

"Noooo!" wailed the rest of us.

"Oh, it's the babies, squealing about nothing again," said a drawling voice right by us. It was the Queen and the Goblin – the M&Ms in other words – leering smugly at us like a couple of Hallowe'en masks.

"Hey, Thomas, I always thought you were a real drip," sneered Emily 'the Goblin' Berryman, nodding at the bucket on Frankie's chair, "but you really proved it today."

A couple of their cronies laughed at this, and it made Frankie fume. "No one could be drippier than you two lamebrains," she said. But the M&Ms had already turned their backs and stalked off across the classroom.

"The M&Ms are asking for it," announced Kenny darkly. "Distract them for me – quick!"

Kenny's always doing this, and it teaches you to think on your feet, I can tell you! I was the one with the inspiration this time. While the others just looked a bit stunned – and Fliss looked nervous too (she worries about Kenny's mad revenge schemes) – I marched over to the bucket on Frankie's chair and, gasping, yelled out, "Emma! Emily! Isn't this your drawing?"

We'd spotted them in other wet breaks

working on an awful picture of Westlife they'd copied out of some soppy magazine. So as soon as they saw me pointing to the bucket, they scrambled across the room like their knickers were on fire.

When they got to me, and saw that I was pointing at nothing but the dirty rainwater collecting in the bottom of the bucket, they snapped, "Oh ha *ha*," really sarkily, and "Can't you come up with anything better than that, Rosie *Po*-sie?"

I wasn't worried at all. I sauntered back to Kenny's desk, where Kenny winked at me and said, "Nice one."

"What did you do?" I asked her, but Kenny just grinned.

Frankie and Fliss shrugged at me, and Lyndz shook her head. It was a mystery to all of us. For the next few minutes we tried to look normal, like we were thinking about other things. But all the time we were holding our breaths with nervous excitement and keeping our attention superglued to the M&Ms. I got eye-ache from squinting sideways at them. The last thing I wanted to do was put them on the alert with outright staring.

"But nothing's happening," whispered Fliss after a while.

"Did you do *anything*, McKenzie?" hissed Frankie. By way of reply, Kenny jabbed her in the ribs with her elbow, and nodded over at Emily Berryman.

The Goblin was reaching down into her bag and fiddling with something inside it. She kept glancing up at Mr Pownall, as if to check he wasn't looking.

The next thing we knew there was a tiny click, and then suddenly – SKWOOSH! Bright pink liquid started spurting from the Goblin's bag like a freaked-out fountain.

"Eeeeiii! Aaaaah!" the Goblin shrieked. She made a dash for the bin, still holding the mad fountain.

"Never knew the Goblin's voice went that high!" said Frankie, who was laughing fit to burst, along with the rest of the class.

"What *is* it?" Fliss spluttered.

"Can... of pink soda..." Kenny managed to say, laughing so hard she could barely speak. "I shook it up!"

Emily's dash for the bin ensured that about six desks and twice as many people got covered in sticky soda. Everyone was squealing – everyone, that is, except for Emma Hughes, who was holding up a sopping wet exercise book. She looked like she was about to cry.

Suddenly we heard a chair scrape back. Mr Pownall stood up, a look of major doom on his face. "Well done, Emily!" he thundered, in a voice that didn't mean 'well done' at all. "What an irresponsible girl you are!"

In a nanosecond, the room went deathly quiet (apart from the odd hiccup from Lyndz). Emily was standing by the bin looking like a damp dishrag.

"Do you know there is a rule against having cans of fizzy drink in the classroom?" said Mr Pownall.

"Yes, Mr Pownall," said Emily softly.

"And *why* do you suppose that is?"

"To stop..." She winced "...*that* happening."

"Exactly," said Mr Pownall. "Which proves just how irresponsible you are. You *knew* the rule and you *deliberately* broke it. Go and fetch a mop and some cloths. And after that you can take yourself to Mrs Poole's office and explain exactly why I have sent you."

As Emily slunk off to get the cleaning stuff, I turned to Kenny and gave her my hundred-watt grin. I would've given her a high five too, but that would've been too obvious. Emma Hughes, dripping with sticky wet soda, was looking daggers at her right that moment. Kenny stared innocently back like butter wouldn't melt in her mouth! The others were desperately trying not to look smug and give the game away. I bet, like me, they were all dying to say "Who's a drip now?" It was cool.

I noticed that Fliss was looking particularly relieved. She always worries that Kenny on the warpath is going to mean serious trouble for us. Little did she know that before long she'd be landed with a double helping – no, *quadruple* helping – of spectacular Kenny-trouble. Poor Fliss. If only one of us could have warned her...

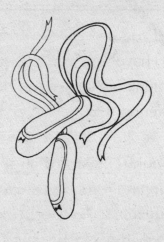

Oops! I'm getting ahead of myself. I shouldn't be talking about Fliss's disaster yet. I must tell you the story in the right order, or the others will be on my back! So, where was I?

Ah, yes. The week of Kenny's sleepover. Well, I was looking forward to that sleepover, big time – and I knew I wouldn't be the only one. But when I met up with the others at school the next morning, Fliss seemed to be in an odd mood. She looked about as happy as a wet weekend.

"Ready for our prancing class, then?" asked Kenny, slapping her on the back.

"Huh? Oh, yeah..." said Fliss uncertainly.

"What's up, Fliss?" said Lyndz, getting all concerned. "Has something happened at home?"

"No," said Fliss. "Well – kind of..." She fiddled with one of her plaits. Then she blurted out, "Mum says we're going skiing in the holidays!"

There was a split second of silence. Then Frankie and Kenny screamed together: "*Skiing*??" And Lyndz said, "But that's a *brilliant* thing!"

"I know it is," said Fliss. "And I'll get a gorgeous tan, Mum says. And we'll have to go shopping for the special clothes and everything..."

Kenny was rolling her eyes by this point. "What's eating you, then?"

"Well, being away for the whole of the time we're off school," said Fliss. "It'll be weird, not seeing you lot. And..." She hesitated. "I've not skiied before, and I'm kind of nervous."

"You're right to be," said Kenny, nodding, and putting on her really serious BBC2 documentary voice. "Skiing is very dangerous. If you don't keep exactly to the right path, you might fall down some hidden ravine. And you'll lie at the bottom with both your legs broken, and no one will be able to hear your cries for help..."

"Kenny, cut it out!" squeaked Lyndz. Fliss looked terrified. Kenny cracked a grin. She wants to be a doctor and loves scaring us with tales of horrific *ER*-type injuries – the gorier the better.

"I'm so jealous!" said Frankie. "Fliss, it'll be brilliant! Are you all going? Callum too?"

Fliss nodded. "There are some little kids' lessons that Callum can go to," she said.

Just then the bell rang, so there was no more time to discuss the hardships of Fliss's luxury holiday – or tomorrow's sleepover, which it struck me we'd hardly planned at all yet.

It turned out that it was going to be our turn for the dance workshop after morning break. When the time came and we'd all got changed, we trooped into the school hall. Some of the class were looking excited, some (the boys and Kenny, mainly) looked like they were about to go to the dentist's.

The dancers – a man and a woman – were already there waiting for us. They were both lean and fit-looking, and were standing up really straight, as if they had broom-handles instead of spines. Their smiles were friendly, though. Still, everyone immediately went shy and started shuffling around the edges of the room.

"I thought they'd be a bit more glamorous," Fliss whispered to me. She had a point. The dancers were dressed in faded, frayed old T-shirts and leggings that my mum would've put in the bin if they'd been mine.

"I'd like to welcome our visitors to Cuddington Primary," Mrs Weaver said, looking a bit flushed. "Children, this is Miss Lorna Baker, and Mr Sean Goldman. I'm sure we'd all like to thank them for giving up their valuable time to be with us."

The bloke, Sean, was pretty good-looking, with very dark curly hair. "D'you reckon Fliss'll fall for the tall dark stranger?" Kenny

25

whispered, nudging me in the ribs. Despite her disappointment about the clothes, Fliss looked bright-eyed and excited.

We tease Fliss quite a lot about boys. She's definitely soppier than the rest of us, mainly about Ryan Scott, this boy in our class she wants to marry when she's older. I mean – Ryan Scott? Yeuch! But that's Fliss for you. I guess she's into romance and hearts and flowers and all that stuff. The rest of us are more into girl power, thank you very much.

I was convinced that Lorna and Sean were going to have us pointing our toes and skipping about, just like Kenny had said. But what we actually did came as a big surprise.

First off, there were a few warm-up stretches. Nothing fancy, just reaching to the ceiling and touching your toes-type stuff. Then we played a game.

"It's called the Newspaper Game," explained Lorna. "First of all you need to find a partner."

The Sleepover Club dived for one another,

of course. But – major problemo. There are five of us! Because of where we were standing, Kenny and Frankie dived for each other and so did Lyndz and I. That left Fliss, of course, looking a bit miz.

"Grab Ryan!" hissed Kenny teasingly, but Lyndz called out, "Come with us in a three!" and seized Fliss's wrist and dragged her over to our corner.

The rest of the class had dived for their best mates too. The M&Ms were standing together smugly (wouldn't you just know it?), and Ryan and Danny, and the other usual pairings, could be spotted all over the room. It turned out that there was an odd number altogether, so there was no one spare for Fliss to partner up with anyway.

"No threes allowed," said Lorna, shaking her head at us.

A second later, I could hardly believe my eyes. There was Sean, the handsome stranger, striding over to Fliss and saying, "I'll be your partner." Fliss blushed right up to the roots of her blonde hair, and looked so pleased you'd think she'd just been asked out by Zac Efron.

Well, Kenny, Frankie, Lyndz and I were all winking at one another madly, as you can imagine. We were nudging each other about the M&Ms, too, who were looking really jealous. They're such teachers' pets! The next minute, though, Lorna started to explain the rules of the game and we all had to concentrate.

The first thing she did was hand every couple a sheet of newspaper. "I've brought some music," she said, brandishing several CDs. "Basically, we're going to have a disco."

"Excellent!" said Lyndz, grinning at me.

"But every so often," Lorna went on, "I'll turn the music off – just like in Musical Chairs. When the music stops, each couple has to stand on their piece of newspaper. If anyone falls off – if your feet touch the floor – you and your partner are out."

"Easy!" I said, as Lyndz and I practised standing on the paper together. There was plenty of room.

"Hang on!" laughed Lorna. "There's a twist. Every time the music starts again, you must fold your paper in half."

Have you ever played this game? It's such a scream! As your piece of paper gets smaller and smaller, you reach the point where one person has to give the other a piggyback, just so that you can both be 'on' the paper without anyone's feet touching the floor. But it doesn't stop there...

Soon Lyndz had me on her back *and* was standing on one foot. All that horse-riding she does must've made her legs super-strong. Even so, she was wobbling all over the place because we were both laughing so much.

Loads of people had dropped out already, and now it was the M&Ms' turn. It was hilarious. Emma Hughes had been doing all the piggyback carrying so far, and while we were dancing, Lyndz and I had heard her complaining that Emily was too heavy. So this time she made Emily carry *her*. Only Emily's much smaller than Emma, of course, so when the music stopped and

Emma took a flying leap on to Emily's back, Emily lost her balance straight away.

"Whoooa!" she shrieked, her face turning purple and her mouth blowing out little desperate puffs as she tried to keep upright.

"Stand up properly!" Emma demanded, just as Emily's legs buckled and she keeled over sideways like those slow-motion films you get of buildings collapsing.

The funniest thing was the way they both sat there arguing about it afterwards.

"You didn't even try!" the Queen was saying.

"I didn't stand a chance – you landed on me like a big lump!" the Goblin growled back.

Honestly, Lyndz and I were shaking with laughter so badly that we were desperate for Lorna to get the music back on as fast as possible, or we would be going the same way...

The next time round Kenny and Frankie were out (Kenny had been dancing so enthusiastically, she got her feet in a tangle and couldn't stay on the bit of paper at all). Then I suddenly realised, looking around, that there were only three couples left: Lyndz and me, Ryan and Danny, and Fliss and Sean.

Lorna put the music on again. By now our piece of paper seemed about the size of a postage stamp – *and* it was thick and springy with being folded so often, so it was extra tricky to balance on. We didn't stand a chance. Never mind the Leaning Tower of Pisa – we were the Collapsing Tower of Cuddington.

Ryan and Danny had managed to stay on their paper, though. And across the other side of the room, Sean was balancing perfectly on the ball of one foot, with Fliss on his back as if she was no more bother than the tiniest, lightest rucksack!

Lorna laughed. "I think we've got a winner," she said, pointing to Ryan and Danny.

"Hey!" complained Sean, holding his hands out to draw attention to his perfect balance.

"Yes, I can see you," said Lorna, "but I don't think I've spotted – what's your name, sweetie?"

"Felicity," squeaked Fliss.

"I haven't spotted Felicity giving Sean a piggyback yet," said Lorna. "So I think you've had an unfair advantage."

"*Right*," said Sean. He let Fliss slither down from his back. Then, all mock-determination, he put his hands on her shoulders and lifted his leg as if he was going to climb on to her!

Fliss giggled and went bright pink again. Sean grinned and reassured her: "Only joking."

But then he did something amazing. Standing behind Fliss he got her to raise one leg at the back – "It's called an arabesque," he said – and then, with one hand under her thigh and the other at her waist, he lifted her till his arms were straight, way above his head.

"Oh my!" exclaimed Mrs Weaver from her chair in the corner, her eyes shining as if she was at some amazing circus show.

"Don't try this at home, kids," said Sean, walking round the room while Fliss emitted little delighted squeaks somewhere near the ceiling.

"Big show off!" laughed Lorna.

Sean grinned, stuck his tongue out at her, and gently lowered Fliss to the floor. By this time Fliss was opening and shutting her mouth like a goldfish. And the M&Ms were positively green, they were so jealous!

After that, the rest of the workshop went like a fab party. The whole class were really into it by now. There were no more games – that had just been to get us in the mood, I think – but we tried making pictures of things with our bodies. Things like anger, or excitement, or sadness. Then, after these still poses (it was a bit like pretending to be statues, I guess) we tried moving to express the same 'feelings'. It was really interesting. Kenny liked 'anger' the best – she stomped around the hall, puffed up like some bizarre, Leicester-City-supporting ogre.

"That was *sooo* wicked!" said Frankie, bouncing about the changing room afterwards.

"We should do the Newspaper Game at our sleepover tomorrow!" said Fliss.

"Hey, yeah!" agreed Lyndz. "But wouldn't that mean we'd need to invite Sean too, to be your partner?" Fliss went beetroot again, which gave the rest of us such a major attack of the giggles that Lyndz got hiccups.

"That's – hic – torn it!" she spluttered.

"Don't worry, we'll cure you!" yelled Kenny. "Pile on, guys!"

And in a second the Sleepover Club was one big mass of arms and legs. "It's a dance called Squeezing Out The Hiccups," said Frankie when Mrs Weaver came in and told us off.

I don't think Mrs Weaver found it funny. But we did.

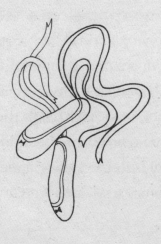

3

"Oh no – look!" Frankie nudged me. "Mrs Poole is making Lorna and Sean eat school dinner. What did they do to deserve *that*?"

I craned my head past the people queuing in front of me, and saw the three of them carrying trays over to one of the tables. "Poor things," I grimaced. "She obviously hates them and wants them never to come back to Cuddington."

As people collected their food there was a massive scramble to sit on Lorna and Sean's table.

The seats filled up in about two seconds flat.

"Surprise, surprise," said Kenny, as we all sat down together at another table nearby (the Sleepover Club was *far* too cool to join in the scrum). "Look who's sucking up big time."

I glanced across and saw that the M&Ms had bagged the plum seats right next to the dancers and were beaming sickly smiles at them.

"I've never seen the M&Ms move so fast," said Lyndz.

"Poor Lorna and Sean. Those smiles are enough to put anyone off their dinner," added Frankie, making sick noises.

"The *food's* enough to put anyone off their dinner," said Fliss, wrinkling her nose. She was fiddling her fork about in her chicken pie as if she was expecting to find a dead beetle in it.

"Ha, ha. They're not even looking at what they're eating," I said, watching as the M&Ms shovelled forkfuls of pie into their mouths without tearing their eyes from their heroes. "Just wait – they'll be spilling it

36

all down their jumpers any minute now."

"Perfect opportunity! This is too good to miss!" said Kenny. She searched around, looking on the floor, and on the windowsill next to our table.

"What're you after?" asked Frankie.

"Aha!" Kenny's hand dived for something on the dusty windowsill. She flashed her open palm under our noses, then strode off towards the M&Ms' table.

"Eeyeuch!" Fliss cringed. "Did you see – a horrible, curled-up dead spider! How can she even pick it up?"

All our eyes were on Kenny. I couldn't hear what she was saying in the hubbub of the dining hall, but I saw her point to the water jug, and someone pass it to her. As she stretched out to reach it she leaned over Emma Hughes' shoulder, and with the quickest craftiest movement – honestly, that girl could do magic tricks! – she flicked the spider on to Emma's plate.

Emma – with her eyes glued to Sean as if he

was some angel – hadn't spotted a thing. And by the time Kenny got back to our table, she couldn't disguise the massive grin spreading over her face.

We counted the seconds: "One elephant, two elephants, three..." before there was an ear-splitting screech and Emma scraped her chair back.

"Pffff – pfffleeuch!" Her tongue was flapping out of her mouth, and she was actually *spitting* on the floor, desperately trying to get rid of the spider.

"What is it?" screeched Emily Berryman.

"Emma! How disgusting!" roared Mrs Poole, looking absolutely horrified. "Get out of the hall – now!"

"But Mrs Poole!" protested Emily. "There was something in her dinner!"

"Out!" commanded Mrs Poole, pointing to the door. I guess she was a bit tense, what with having guests and wanting the school to look good. Emma ran out of the room, her hands clapped over her mouth.

We were all laughing into our dinners by

then, Kenny hardest of all. A minute later I saw Emily Berryman watching us, a look of anger and then determination creeping over her face like some dark shadow.

"Uh-oh," I said. "The Goblin's on to us."

"It'll be payback time," said Fliss flatly. "And there are two things they'll want to get back at us for. The fizzy drink and now this."

"Aw, we're not scared. Let 'em do their worst," said Kenny, all gung-ho and couldn't-care-less. "We'll take them on any time."

The bravest cowboy in the West – that's Kenny for you!

Later in the lunch break, I'd just been to the school library and was heading back across the playground, looking for the others, when Alana Banana came up to me. "Where's Laura?" she asked.

"Kenny? Er... I'm not sure," I said, looking around. "Maybe she's in the loos."

Alana seemed to hesitate for a moment. Then she said, "Rosie, I was in the changing room just now and I saw some of your P.E. kit on the floor."

"Mine?" I said. I *thought* I could remember putting all my kit in my gym bag after the workshop. But I'd kind of done it on automatic pilot, because I was so busy talking to my friends, so I couldn't be 100% sure.

Alana nodded. "I'd go and get it if I were you, or it'll end up in Lost Property."

"Yeah. Thanks," I said. And Alana ran off across the playground.

I headed straight for the changing room. I hate losing stuff at school. It's such a trauma trying to get it back, and you always get a massive lecture.

Luckily I didn't run into any teachers on the way, and as I came up to the changing room I could see it was empty.

I hurried through the door. And that's when I saw it.

Dangling from the ceiling, limp and pale and lifeless, was a human arm. Dripping with blood. The blood was oozing down it slowly, ending in a great big drop hanging from one of the fingertips.

I screamed. My stomach contracted at the same time like I was going to be sick, and I had to hold on to one of the coat racks to keep my balance.

"Rosie? What is it? Are you OK?" In a second Frankie was by my side. She must have been passing in the corridor and heard me. Was that a piece of luck.

I grabbed hold of her and pointed a trembling finger towards the arm. Frankie gasped and clapped her hand over her mouth, probably to stop herself from screaming too.

"I-I'll fetch a teacher," she stammered. But she hadn't gone more than a couple of steps when a voice shouted out:

"Dur-brains!"

"Who said that?" I looked around. Then I

heard cackling laughter coming from above.

The horrible arm had vanished and a face had appeared in its place, upside down, with the hair dangling round it. It was Emma Hughes. And out from a bundle of coats in the corner came Emily Berryman, laughing like a drain.

I felt sick now in a different way.

"Ha, *ha*! Can't believe you fell for it!" Emma sneered triumphantly. "Who's a poor ickle scaredy-cat, running to get teacher, eh?"

"I *am* going to get a teacher," said Frankie. Normally she wouldn't dream of telling on anyone, even the M&Ms, so I knew she'd been really frightened. She added, "You're not supposed to be up there."

Emma had climbed through the small square hatch in the changing-room ceiling – the one that opens into the loft. She must have lain down up there and dangled her arm through the hole.

"Too late," said Emma. Her face disappeared and her legs popped out instead. She let herself down gingerly on to the nearest free-standing coat rack. It wobbled a lot as she pulled the hatch cover shut.

"Well, help me down, then!" she snapped at the Goblin, who started forward and tried to hold one of Emma's ankles. Emma kicked it free irritably, so the Goblin held the coat rack instead and promptly got her fingers trodden on.

"Ouch!"

"I couldn't see where you were, could I?" said Emma crossly. Now, up close, I could see that she'd whitened her arm with talc, and the 'blood' had been tomato ketchup that she must have pinched from the dining room.

By this time the M&Ms were squabbling so much, Frankie and I were grinning, though we still felt a bit shaky. "Come on," Frankie whispered. "Let's leave them to it." And we legged it down the corridor and back out into the playground.

There we found Lyndz and Kenny, trying to put a zig-zag parting in Fliss's hair.

"Aw, that hurts!" Fliss was squealing.

"Hold still!" said Kenny firmly. When she saw

43

us, she asked, "Does this look right to you? I'm not sure what I'm doing, to be honest."

"Speak for yourself," said Lyndz, comb poised in mid-air. "Where've you two been? You look white as anything."

And when Frankie and I started to say what had happened, all three of them forgot Fliss's new hairstyle and listened, open-mouthed.

"And was the blood like... dripping on the *floor*?" asked Kenny at last.

"Don't even *say* blood!" said Fliss, looking queasy. "It was *ketchup*."

"Whatever it was, it must've been scary," said Lyndz, putting an arm round me.

"They must've planned it for you, Kenny," I said. "The first thing Alana said was that she was looking for you. It was only when she couldn't find you that she must've thought I'd do instead."

"Too bad," said Kenny. "I would've loved it! Great practice for when I'm a doctor. Mind you," she added, "I wish I'd thought of it first. It was a mean trick to pull on you non-medical types. Those creeps are so for it now!"

I grinned. What's that Three Musketeers motto? *All for one and one for all.* Well, that's just like the Sleepover Club – and it was good to know it, after the shock I'd just had. That afternoon we were going to be watching Lorna and Sean's dancing demonstration. But somehow I knew that however brilliant it was, the Sleepover Club would have something else on their minds. Now it wasn't just Kenny who'd be thinking of revenge.

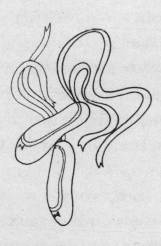

The demonstration *was* brilliant. And actually, I have to be honest with you: it did drag my thoughts away from the M&Ms a bit. But that's no bad thing. Sometimes I don't think they deserve the thinking time we give them!

At home after school, when Mum was back from picking up Adam, I was bubbling with news about Lorna and Sean – what ace fun we'd had in the workshop, and how amazing their demonstration had been.

"It was *sooo* fantastic!" I said, leaping round the kitchen, and leaning on the back of Adam's wheelchair to try and stand on my toes.

"Hey, don't tip him over!" scolded Mum, but Adam was laughing at me and didn't look as if he minded at all.

"They were wearing proper costumes. The woman had a sticky-out skirt on, made of net..."

"A tutu," said Mum.

"... and it had glittery bits all over it," I went on, "and from the audience in a theatre they look like real jewels but when you get up close – Lorna let us have a good look – you can see they're fake. Close-up, the costume even looked kind of... tacky, I suppose. A bit worn, and the material wasn't very nice."

"And what was the dancing like?" asked Mum.

"Totally, totally awesome," I said. "They did part of *Sleeping Beauty*, I think it was. Lorna did all these pirouettes on pointe..."

Adam was frowning at me, looking puzzled.

"... that's spinning round on the tips of your

toes," I explained. "And Sean lifted her loads of times, high in the air. And he did incredible jumps too. His feet went like this..." And I criss-crossed my hands really fast to show Mum what I meant.

"Did the whole school like it?" asked Mum.

"Pretty much. And I think Fliss has decided she wants to be a ballerina now instead of a model," I said. "She's even started walking with her toes pointing sideways, like a duck!"

This made Adam laugh so much he shook. He may have trouble speaking, my brother (he has cerebral palsy, as I expect you know) but he sure can laugh!

Just then the phone rang. "I'll get it!" I said and raced to pick it up. I figured it might be one of the Sleepover Club – and I was right.

"Hey, Rosie." I heard Kenny's voice coming down the line. "Just calling to remind you about the sleepover tomorrow."

"As if I would've forgotten!" I said, in mock outrage. "Have we got a theme?"

"Not really. I guess we've left it a bit late,"

said Kenny. "I did think we could all dress up for different winter sports, in honour of Fliss going skiing, but no one's got the right gear."

"Winter sports?" I repeated. "You mean like skating and ice hockey and things like that?"

"Yep," said Kenny.

"I haven't a clue what I'd wear."

"Well, me neither. So just bring your usual stuff. And I reckon we'll have enough to do plotting revenge on the M&Ms, anyway."

Which sounded likely to me. And as it turned out, we had even more to plan than we'd expected.

The next morning – Friday – Mrs Poole made an announcement in Assembly.

"Most of you will have noticed by now that parts of the school roof are in a very bad state," she said. I glanced at Frankie, who was sitting next to me. *She* certainly knew. Her chair still had a bucket on it.

"A new roof costs a great deal of money," Mrs Poole went on, "and to raise that money I need the help of everyone at Cuddington Primary. Pupils..." she looked round the hall. "...teachers, even mums and dads."

"I knew it," muttered Frankie. "Sponsored spells, maths marathons, ugh!" Down at the end of our row Mrs Weaver's head turned. Her teacher radar had sensed someone Talking In Assembly (a major sin in Weaver's book), but she couldn't make out who it was. Frankie zipped her lips tight shut.

"Our first fund-raising event is something I hope we can all be enthusiastic about," Mrs Poole was saying. "On the last day of term we're going to have a party!"

A ripple of excitement ran round the hall. Mrs Poole beamed. "I'd like each class to help make the decorations and plan the entertainments," she said, "and we'll sell tickets to as many mums and dads, grans and grandpas and aunts and uncles as we can.

There'll be raffles and competitions and lots more to tempt people along."

When we got back to our classroom everyone was talking at once about the party.

"Do you think we'll play games?" said Fliss. "Imagine Pass the Parcel with the *whole school*!"

"It'd be the biggest parcel ever!" giggled Lyndz, spreading her arms out wide. "You'd have to roll it along like a giant snowball."

"I vote for Pin the Tail on the Donkey," said Frankie, with a mischievous glint in her eye. "Only instead of a donkey, use the M&Ms!" She clutched her bottom and started leaping around, shrieking "Ow! Ouch!" as if someone was trying to stick pins in her.

Well, that was it. Frankie looked so hilarious, bouncing about like a half-mad pixie, that the rest of us completely lost it. Lyndz started hiccupping, I giggled so much I got a stitch, and Kenny tripped over her bag and ended up sprawled on the floor, still laughing.

"Settle down, now!" bawled Mrs Weaver

over the noise, clapping her hands. "And do get up, Laura! Nothing is *that* funny." (Which just goes to show what a hopeless sense of humour teachers have. Frankie was *definitely* that funny.)

Kenny hauled herself into her chair, wiping her cheeks with the back of her sleeve. Lyndz, I could see, was holding her breath against the hiccups. Meanwhile Emma Hughes, in her best goody-goody voice, was asking, "How can we help prepare for the party, Mrs Weaver?"

"Well, Emma, along with Mr Pownall's class, our main job is to decorate the hall," Mrs Weaver replied. "The party is in three weeks' time, so we'll spend our Art lessons between now and then working on our decorations.

"But that's not all." Mrs Weaver walked round and sat on the edge of her desk, which is what she does when she's feeling chatty. "Lorna and Sean from the British National Ballet have kindly agreed to be guests of honour at the party," she said. "And you all did so well in their workshop that I thought this was too good an opportunity to miss. So – I'd like you to get yourselves into groups, and make up your own dance routines. On the morning of the last day of term we'll have a competition, with Lorna and Sean as the judges. The winners will perform in front of everyone at the party."

"Fantastic!" whispered Lyndz, her eyes as big as saucers. Her hiccups, I could tell, had suddenly vanished.

"To make sure no one's left out," said Mrs Weaver, "I'd like to know by the end of today who's going to be in each group."

"We'll be a group, right? Us five?" said Fliss, flapping a hand at the usual sleepover suspects.

"Don't be thick! Of course we will!" said Frankie.

Over the other side of the classroom I saw the M&Ms huddle together with their heads down low, whispering. When they straightened up again, they were looking so smug and self-satisfied, it made me feel queasy.

"Smug attack at 3 o'clock!" I whispered to Kenny. Kenny looked round. To show what she thought of the M&Ms she made a face, crossing her eyes and lolling her tongue out.

As soon as the bell rang for break, we started talking about the dance competition. "Listen, guys," said Kenny, beckoning us into a quiet corner of the playground. "This is serious. We *have* to win it. We have to beat the M&Ms!"

Frankie nodded. "It'll be the perfect revenge."

"They deserve to come *last* after what they did to you and Rosie," said Fliss.

"We'll have to practise loads," I said.

"Too right," said Kenny. "We can start making plans tonight at the sleepover. Bring all your best ideas. It'll be a council of war!"

It was great to feel we had a really important project on the go. I couldn't wait for the sleepover. When I got home, I parked my bag by the front door ages before Fliss and her mum were due to pick me up. I was getting a lift with them to Kenny's because it was one of Mum's nights for being late home from college. That was why my sister Tiffany was in the kitchen right this second, complaining about having to come straight home after school to look after me and Adam.

After tea I watched at the window for Fliss's car, and was up and out before either she or her mum could get as far as ringing the doorbell. "See ya! Wouldn't wanna beee ya!" I yelled to Tiff, who was upstairs giving herself a face pack (basically smearing loads of smelly mud on her face – bleurgh!), and banged the door behind me.

"I've got *so* many ideas for the routine!" said Fliss, her eyes shining, as I opened the car door and slid on to the back seat beside her. "I would tell you now – but I guess I'd better save them till we get there. How about you?"

"Er... I've got loads too," I said, nodding

vigorously. To be honest with you, I hadn't. I'm not much good at making things up on my own. For some reason it's miles better when I'm actually with the gang, and we're all shouting out ideas at once.

When we got to Kenny's, the door was opened by her mum, who told us to go straight through to the garage. That's where Kenny keeps her pet rat, Merlin, since she's not allowed to keep him in her bedroom.

"Yeuch! I'm not going in there with that thing!" whispered Fliss, clutching her rolled-up sleeping bag as if it were a magic charm to ward off rodents.

The McKenzies have a normal-sized door that leads from the kitchen into the garage, as well as the big tip-up garage door. Fliss stood on the threshold of the kitchen door, wobbling her feet back and forth over the ridge of the door-frame. I'd gone ahead of her into the garage, though I must admit I didn't go very near Merlin's cage.

56

"I thought this would be a good rehearsal space," said Kenny, flinging her arms out and spinning round. "We'll make it the coolest, wickedest, funkiest routine we've ever done." She strutted across the grimy garage floor, and struck a pose like a model, one hip stuck out to the side.

I burst out laughing. My breath billowed out of my mouth in ghostly clouds.

"It's pretty cold in here," said Fliss, shivering.

"Too right – it's an icebox!" said Frankie, appearing at my shoulder. "Let's come and work it out in here when we know a bit more what we're doing. We haven't even talked about ideas yet. Hey – where's Lyndz?"

"Behind you!" We spun round to find Lyndz next to Fliss in the doorway.

Kenny yelled, "All present and correct!" like a sergeant major. Then she bombed back into the house at a million miles an hour and pounded up the stairs, shouting, "Follow me to my HQ!"

Up in her bedroom we found packets of

crisps and popcorn, fizzy drinks and biscuits in a heap on her sister's bed.

"Is Molly out all night?" I asked.

Kenny nodded. "She's sleeping at her friend Janice's house – so we can do what we like!" She leapt on to Molly's duvet and started bouncing up and down.

"Hey! You're crunching the crisps!" said Fliss. Some of the packets were going flying, others were getting trampolined. Kenny kicked her feet out in front of her and landed on her bottom. "Right," she said, getting her breath back. "Let's make a start."

"I'm going to write down all our ideas and the things we'll need," said Frankie, diving into her overnight bag and bringing out a really cool purple notepad and a matching pen.

"Well, I think we should do a ballet," said Fliss.

"You have to be joking," said Kenny, reaching for a crisp packet, and tossing a couple more to Lyndz and me.

"No, think about it." Fliss's face was serious.

"Lorna and Sean aren't just dancers, they're *ballet* dancers, right? So what's their favourite type of dance?"

"Baffuff," said Lyndz with her mouth full. "Sorry..." she swallowed, "...ballet."

"Right," said Fliss. "And what d'you think they'll like most at the competition?"

"You've got a point," said Frankie, chewing the end of her purple pen thoughtfully. "But the problem is, ballet's really complicated. And none of us knows how to do it. Just think of those steps Lorna and Sean did at the demonstration."

"If we want to win," said Fliss, "we have to give ourselves the best chance. And anyway, I go to ballet lessons. I could be the swan queen at the front and you lot could be my corps de ballet."

"Corr de what?" asked Kenny.

"The ones who stand at the back," explained Fliss.

Kenny grinned. "Ahhh, *now* I see why you want to do a ballet. You want to be the star!"

"No!" Fliss said, turning pink. "I'm just trying to think up a good plan, that's all."

"We need to choose something we can all do really well," I said. I had a big bottle of cola between my knees and I was opening it really slowly – *fzzzzzzz* – so it wouldn't spurt everywhere like the Goblin's soda. "Let's face it, we're competing against the M&Ms, not Lorna and Sean. And the M&Ms are hardly going to be putting on *Swan Lake*, are they?"

"Rosie's right," said Lyndz. "Sorry, Fliss, but I think ballet's out."

"OK," said Fliss brightly. I was surprised she wasn't huffy, considering we'd all just shouted down her idea. Then straight away she said, "How about I be Gwen Stefani, and you four can be my backing dancers?"

"Nooooo!" the rest of us squealed together.

"But a pop routine's a really good idea," said Frankie.

"What's wrong with Gwen Stefani?" asked Fliss.

"Nothing," said Lyndz patiently, "but it'd be better if we were all equal, like in the Sugababes or Girls Aloud. Don't you think?"

"Hey, Sugababes!" I said. "We could be Sleepoverbabes!"

"That's absolutely brilliant!" grinned Frankie, writing it down. "We've got a name, then. That's a good start."

"I tell you what we should definitely have," said Kenny. "Those cool microphone headsets they wear – you know, the ones that wrap round your head, with a tiny microphone sticking out by your mouth."

"Oh, ace, Kenny," said Frankie, raising an eyebrow. "Are you going rob a bank to pay for them, or has your mum just won the lottery?"

"Ha, *ha*," said Kenny. "I didn't mean real ones. We could make fake ones – out of wire or something. It would look so wicked!"

"It would, too!" said Lyndz. "What could we use? Coathanger wire or something?"

"Wait a sec." Kenny bounded over to the wardrobe. She pulled out one of Molly's dresses, slipped it off its hanger and chucked the dress back in the cupboard. Then she took the coathanger and tried to bend it over her head by pulling the two ends down. "Nnnnrrrgh!" Her face screwed up with the effort. "Ooof! It doesn't half hurt!"

"Hmm, I think the wire's too thick," said Lyndz.

"And the ends are too sharp," said Fliss. "It'd be dangerous. We could cut our mouths or something."

"That's a shame," said Frankie. "It *was* a cool idea, Kenny."

"How about garden wire?" I said. "You know – that stuff people use when they want a plant to grow up a cane. It's quite thin, and it's covered in plastic, which might make it less scratchy."

"Perfect!" exclaimed Kenny. "I'll go and ask Mum if we've got any."

She dashed off, and was back a few minutes later with a whole roll of green-coloured wire. Unlike the coathanger, it was really easy to bend, and you could twist several pieces together if you wanted a thicker strip.

After a few false starts, Frankie was the first to make a really good headband, with a little arm attached that curved down to her mouth.

"You need a blob at the end for the microphone," I said.

"How about glueing on a Smartie?" suggested Lyndz.

"I'd spend my whole time trying to eat it," said Frankie, sticking out her tongue as if there was a Smartie just out of reach.

It took us the whole evening making headsets for everyone, but it was worth it. They looked amazing. None of us wanted to take them off, even when we'd changed into our pyjamas and were snuggled inside our sleeping bags.

"Ground control to Major Rosie," said Lyndz.

"Roger, ground control," I replied.

"This is Houston..." intoned Kenny. "Astronaut Frankie, do you read me?"

"Loud and clear!" said Frankie. "Guys, we

are so cool! The M&Ms won't have a hope against us!"

I was sure she was right. Little did we know, though, that the M&Ms were cooking up some major plans of their own. But we would soon find out.

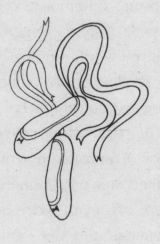

On Monday morning Kenny was the last of the Sleepover Club to arrive at school. As soon as she got through the gate the rest of us leapt on her.

"Ace sleepover, Kenny!" yelled Frankie.

"Taken your headset off yet?" giggled Lyndz.

The best thing had been catching sight of Kenny on Saturday morning. She'd fallen asleep with her headset on, and when she woke up it was squashed into a weird shape, and she had a bright red stripe on her cheek where she'd been lying on the wire.

Now Kenny growled in mock annoyance and launched herself on to Lyndz's back. "Right, Collins!" she bawled. "Horseback punishment! Giddy-up, there!"

"The only thing is..." shouted Fliss, above the noise of Lyndz whinnying and galloping round, and Kenny bawling out the Lone Ranger theme tune, "the thing is... we still haven't got anywhere with the actual routine."

"Shhh! Keep it down!" hissed Frankie, twitching her head in the direction of the playground railings, where the M&Ms were standing with Alana Palmer. From the way they were all waving their arms about, it looked like they were talking about the competition too.

"I thought of that," said Kenny, jumping down from Lyndz's back. "And here's what we do. It's a two-pronged attack. One: keep our eyes and ears and everything else peeled for any sign – *anything* – that gives us a clue what those two snotty saddos are planning. And two: we hold an emergency meeting at break, round by the bins."

"Top plan, Captain Kenny!" said Frankie and we all did high fives.

At break time Lyndz and I went to the loos. As we were hurriedly washing our hands, not wanting to be late for our emergency meeting, we heard voices coming from behind two of the cubicle doors.

"It's just going to make our routine so special," said a gruff voice. "No one will even think of doing the same as us."

I nudged Lyndz. She mouthed "The Goblin?", and I nodded and pressed a finger to my lips.

"Of course not," came the other voice, which belonged to the Queen, sounding really snooty as usual. "We're leagues ahead of everyone else anyway. There won't *be* any competition!"

The next moment we heard the sound of

flushing and, quick as a flash, Lyndz and I bolted out of the toilets. We didn't want the M&Ms coming out and finding that we'd been eavesdropping.

"What d'you reckon it is, this thing that's going to make their routine so special?" I said, as we dashed round the gym block and headed towards the giant school bins.

Suddenly Lyndz stopped dead in her tracks. I had to run back to her to see what was the matter.

"You know what?" she said, clutching at my sleeve and looking really alarmed. "It sounds like they've got some sort of secret weapon!"

"Secret weapon???"

We'd blurted it out as soon as we'd got to the bins, and now Frankie, Kenny and Fliss were looking at us like we'd just told them the world was going to end in five minutes. Lyndz and I were both panting from having run so fast, but the others were breathing through their mouths too, because the bins smelt so disgusting. Meeting by the bins wasn't half pongy, but it was brilliant when you wanted to keep something secret, as no one usually liked to hang around there.

"But it's a dance competition not, like, a fight or anything!" said Fliss.

"Durr! They don't mean a *weapon* weapon," said Frankie impatiently. "It must be some mega-amazing idea for their routine."

"We're doomed!" said Lyndz.

"Don't be so wet," growled Kenny. "We haven't even started yet. Come on, guys. Don't let them rattle us."

"We need to arrange a proper rehearsal," said Fliss, "so we can make up our routine. Break time isn't enough."

"OK, so what about this weekend?" suggested Kenny. "Saturday, for instance? We could spend the whole day on it."

"Mmm." I frowned. "I've got to go to Safeway's with my mum in the morning. I can't get out of it. She needs a hand, especially since Adam's decided to come with us this week."

"And I'll be at the stables in the morning," said Lyndz.

"The afternoon, then?" said Frankie. "We need somewhere with lots of space. It's a shame it's too cold to rehearse outside."

"Don't even think about it," said Fliss, shivering and hopping about from one foot to the other. I think Fliss must be more delicate than the rest of us. She really suffers, having to be outside at break time in the winter.

"How are you going to manage on holiday, Fliss, being out on the ski slopes all day?" I asked.

"Oh, I'll be fine," said Fliss confidently. "On Saturday my mum bought me some *gorgeous* pink salopets."

"What are salo—... salo—... whatever you said?" spluttered Kenny.

"It's this dead cool jumpsuit that's padded, kind of like a sleeping bag," said Fliss.

Kenny pulled a face. "Sounds *sooo* elegant – not!"

"They are, too!" Fliss insisted.

Suddenly the bell went.

"OK, guys!" said Lyndz quickly, holding up her hands like a referee. "Decision time. This rehearsal. How about we have it at my house on Saturday afternoon? I'll need to ask permission, but I don't suppose Mum and Dad'll mind. We could use the sitting room. It's pretty big when you push all the furniture back."

"That'd be perfect," said Frankie, writing it down.

A few moments later, when we were lining up, ready to troop back into the classroom, I whispered to Lyndz, "I still wish we knew what the M&Ms were up to. I wish we could read their minds."

Lyndz nodded. Then she said, "Hey, maybe we could! If we all sat round a table and concentrated really hard, and held hands and things..."

"Yeuch!" whispered Frankie. "Can you imagine all the rubbish that's swilling round in those two saddos' skulls? Wading through

71

that stuff would be like going through those stinky bins with our bare hands."

Lyndz and I giggled. "Gross!"

Have you ever been to Lyndz's house? It's a crazy place! Lyndz's dad is doing it up. He's even moving whole rooms and staircases and things. Only, he's been doing it up ever since I've been friends with Lyndz, and he never seems nearer to finishing. Whenever I go round to Lyndz's house, I expect the unexpected. I don't think I'd be surprised to see the front door half way up the wall!

It was an ace venue for our Sleepoverbabes rehearsal, though, because I knew we'd be able to leap about and Lyndz's mum and dad wouldn't mind. There's always so much building grunge in the house that there's no way they can be precious and tell you to sit still in case you mess the place up.

When I got there, Lyndz had already lugged the sitting-room furniture to the edges of the room, with the help of her older brothers, Stuart and Tom.

"They're not going to stay and watch, are they?" I hissed to Lyndz. I knew I'd feel really shy, rehearsing in front of them.

"No way!" Lyndz hissed back. "A complete Brother Ban will be in force this afternoon."

Which was a good job, since Lyndz doesn't have just those two older brothers – she has two younger ones as well!

A few minutes later Fliss made a grand entrance waving a dvd. "Guess what?" she said. "Girls Aloud were on TV this morning and they did a seriously awesome routine. I recorded it."

"Why don't we start off watching that, then?" suggested Lyndz. "To see if we can get some ideas."

Fliss was right, the routine was awesome. But it was one thing to watch it and go "Wow!", and quite another to work out exactly how to do the steps. It took us ages just to get two or three. We used the pause button so many times, Lyndz was worried that the dvd player would explode!

But what we saw gave us ideas of our own, too, and we ended up with loads of fab moves. There was the bum wiggle, for instance, and the shoulder pop, the kick-and-turn, and the 'cross your heart', named by Frankie (which involved sticking your hands out in front of you – right, left – and then crossing them – right, left – on your chest).

"We are *so* cool!" giggled Frankie, as she and Fliss did a sequence of moves in unison.

'Cool' might have been the right word to describe the other four but, to be honest, 'hot and flustered' was how i felt. I found it so confusing. Sometimes you had to concentrate really hard on moving only one part of your body at a time – your arms, then your shoulders, then your feet – and sometimes you had to move everything at once. I often felt like I had four hands and three feet, at *least*!

"I reckon we should do the choruses all together," said Frankie, "and then, in the verses, one of us comes to the front each time, and does our own thing."

"What kind of 'own thing'?" I asked. Even the idea of standing at the front on my own made my stomach lurch like a rollercoaster ride. I may have played Cinderella in our school panto once, but I still got major stage fright.

"I'll help you, Rosie," said Fliss, who must've noticed how worried I was. "Look – why don't you go: step, kick, shoulder, shoulder, head roll, turn around?" she suggested, doing the moves as she spoke.

"Errrr..." I said uncertainly. "What was that again?"

"OK." Fliss gave a little sigh. "Much slower this time..."

"Nooooo! Shoulder, shoulder, *then* head roll!"

When I'd got it wrong for the seventy-ninth time, I was so frustrated I felt like bursting into tears.

"You have to do it with attack, Rosie!" said Fliss.

"What d'you mean?" I said. To tell you the truth, I was a bit annoyed. It was all right for Fliss – she been going to dancing lessons since she was tiny, so she was used to this sort of thing. I felt like I was making a right idiot of myself.

"Your hands look like wet lettuces! And you're turning too slowly, like some old biddy!" She demonstrated a shuffling, wobbly turn, and it made the others fall about laughing.

That was it. I felt this sudden tight anger in my stomach, and my eyes went swimmy with hot tears. "Well, maybe you should all do it without me, then!" I blurted out, and marched out of the room.

There's a problem having a strop in someone else's house: you don't know where to go. I didn't dare try upstairs in case I bumped into Tom or Stuart, but when you've marched out of a room, you've got to march *to* somewhere, or you're going to look a real berk. So I stomped through the kitchen (which was empty, thank goodness), and straight out of the back door.

Bad move. I'd forgotten how cold it would be in the garden. Luckily Lyndz came looking for me straight away.

"Are you OK?" she said softly, hooking her arm through mine. "Fliss didn't mean to upset you."

"I know." I managed to smile, though my tummy still felt knotty. "I'm fine. I just got a bit frustrated, that's all."

When I got back into the sitting room, Fliss gave my hand a friendly squeeze, and said, "Brilliant! You've got it!" when I went through the steps again. Soon I was feeling much better.

"That's one majorly cool routine we've got there," said Kenny, when we'd run the whole thing from start to finish, including all the new solos.

"We are ace, we are cool, we so completely rule!" chanted Frankie, who'd flopped next to Lyndz on the sofa.

We *were* cool – but boy, did I have a lot of practising to do at home! Luckily, my bedroom's quite big, so I could go through my moves without Tiff watching and laughing at me. That would've really done for my confidence.

On Sunday I practised all morning. I was really keen not to let the others down.

"Rosieeeeeeeee!"

I was vaguely aware that Tiff was yelling up the stairs, but I was determined to get to the end of the chorus section if it killed me.

Just as I made it to the end (with, for the first time, no mistakes!!!), my bedroom door was flung open. Tiff's face appeared, looking annoyed. "Hey, deafo, didn't you hear? It's the phone for you."

I bounded down the stairs and picked up the receiver.

"Hello?"

"Rosie! Thank goodness you're there," said Fliss in a weird breathless voice. "There's been a disaster."

"What? What?" I said. I had sudden vague imaginings of someone being hurt – maybe Lyndz had gone riding... "What's happened?" I almost yelled, clutching the phone so hard my knuckles went white.

"They've changed the flights for our skiing holiday," said Fliss, in a voice of doom, like she was announcing the end of the world.

I had to turn my yelp of laughter into a cough. "Oh, um, dear," I said. "Is it a problem?"

"That's only the biggest understatement of the year!" wailed Fliss. "We're going to have to fly out on the last day of term. I won't be able to go to the party. We'll all have to pull out of the competition. Sleepoverbabes is officially cancelled!"

Friends are tricky, sometimes. I always think it's odd how someone you really, really like can make you so cross that for a moment you even feel you hate them. Or, sometimes, a friend thinks something you just don't agree with – but even though you know they're being silly, you can kind of see how they feel at the same time. Do you know what I mean?

That was what it was like at school the next week with Fliss. She was really upset that the rest of us were going ahead with the competition without her.

"What do you expect us to do?" said Kenny. "All go into mourning cos you're off on some swanky holiday?"

"Yes," said Fliss stubbornly. "I didn't *ask* to go."

"We'd much rather you were there," said Lyndz soothingly. "Of course we would. It won't be the same without you."

"I can't believe you're just going to carry on, like you don't care!" Fliss's eyes filled with tears.

"Oh, get over it," said Kenny bluntly. I could see she'd lost all patience with Fliss.

We were in an Art lesson, working on our decorations for the school hall. Of course, since the decorations were for the party, that was what was on everyone's mind. I could see that for Fliss, it kind of rubbed salt in the wound, as my mum would say. But at the same time I agreed with Kenny. Why did Fliss expect us to bin all our hard work and miss out on the fun of the dance competition just because she was off having an ace time skiing and staying in a posh hotel?

Still, I was trying to keep out of the argument. I

reckoned I'd caused enough trouble, throwing that strop at Lyndz's house. I kept my head down and concentrated on my paper lantern. I was painting it red, with yellow blobs round the edges. In the middle of the yellow blobs I was going to stick scrunched up cellophane sweet wrappers, to look like jewels. It was going to be cool.

"Mum said I could have an extra-special sleepover, to make up for missing the party," said Fliss. "But I'm not sure I want to invite any of you to it, any more."

"Fine," muttered Kenny. "Won't be much of a sleepover on your own."

But a minute later Lyndz said gently, "A sleepover would be so great, Fliss. What kind were you planning? Was it going to have a theme?"

Fliss nodded, smiling despite herself. "Mum came up with it."

"What is it?" I asked.

Now Fliss looked positively excited. "Grease," she said.

"Grease?" said Kenny. "What d'you mean?

Engine oil? Chip fat? What're you talking about?"

"Not grease," said Fliss. "*Grease*. You know, that film with John Travolta."

"Never heard of it," said Kenny.

"It *is* quite old," said Frankie. "But it's cool. Me and Mum got it out from Blockbusters once."

"It's set in this American high school in the Fifties," explained Fliss.

"Prehistoric," said Kenny.

Fliss took no notice. I could see she was really into the idea. "There are these different gangs," she said. "The girls are called the Pink Ladies and they have pink jackets with writing on the back, and they are *so* cool—"

"And the songs are good, too," put in Frankie, dabbling her paintbrush in the water jar.

"Anyhow, my mum said we can have all-American food, like popcorn and hot dogs and milkshakes and stuff," said Fliss.

"Yummy!" said Lyndz.

"That's more like it!" Kenny said, looking brighter.

"And we all have to dress up," Fliss added.

"Well, I'm gonna need some help," said Kenny. "Since I still don't have a clue what you're talking about."

"It's like the original *High School Musical*," said Frankie, in a sing-song voice you'd use to a baby. "Why don't you google it?"

Kenny growled and, picking up her paintbrush, flicked a fine spray of red paint into Frankie's hair. Frankie squealed; giggling, she did it back, with blue.

But it wasn't their lucky day.

"Francesca and Laura!" thundered Mrs Weaver's voice. "Outside the door! Now!"

"Just when the fun was starting," muttered Kenny with a shrug as she walked past.

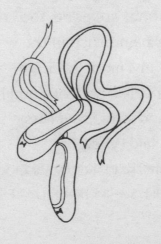

7

The next Saturday Mum helped me pick out my clothes for Fliss's sleepover. We chose some light blue leggings, a denim mini that she'd bought me last summer, a long-sleeved T-shirt with a scoop neck, and my flat black pumps. Mum did my hair in a ponytail, and tidied the wisps with a couple of sparkly clips that Tiffany had lent me.

"Lose them and you're in big trouble," Tiff had said. Sisters – charming, huh?

Now Mum turned me round. "As a finishing touch," she said, "you should have a neck scarf!" She produced a little silk scarf that Gran had given her once, but that she'd never worn.

"Mu-*um*!" I complained. "It'll look naff!"

"No, it won't," said Mum firmly, fixing it round my neck with the knot at the side. She pulled me over to the mirror. "Look – that's proper Fifties style, that is."

And I had to admit that it did look quite cool.

Down in the sitting room I did a twirl for Adam, who gave me a big approving grin. Then Mum took me in the car round to Fliss's.

When Mrs Sidebotham answered the door I could hardly believe my eyes. She had dressed up too! She was wearing a bright yellow, really full skirt, with loads of petticoats underneath, topped with a wide shiny black belt, which she'd nipped in really tightly to make her waist look dead small. Her clingy top was yellow, to match the skirt, and she had her hair in a ponytail like mine. But it was her feet that surprised me the most. Have you ever seen a mum in frilly ankle socks? Well, that's just what Mrs Sidebotham had on, plus a pair of white pumps that were so clean they looked like she'd gone over them with toothpaste.

"You look great, Mrs Sidebotham!" I said as I took off my coat.

"That's very sweet of you, Rosie," replied Fliss's mum, patting her hair. As I bent down to take off my shoes (it's one of the rules of Fliss's house: no shoes indoors) she added, "As a special concession you can keep your shoes on today. I realise that they're part of your costume."

In the sitting room I discovered Fliss, looking like an exact replica of her mum, except that her top and skirt were pink. Kenny was there too, in a Leicester City shirt (surprise, surprise), and jeans.

"Nice outfit, McKenzie," I laughed.

"Blue jeans are very Fifties," she said. "Apparently."

When Lyndz arrived it turned out she was in

jeans too, and a leather jacket that Tom had lent her. I could tell Fliss was a bit disappointed – she had hoped everyone would wear girly things, like her. So it was a relief when Frankie turned up in a madly flowery dress, with bangles on her wrists and her hair in bunches.

"Dad spotted the dress in a charity-shop window," she said, holding the skirt out to the sides and doing a wobbly curtsey.

Just then Andy, Fliss's Mum's boyfriend, came in with a tray of luscious-looking milkshakes and we all cheered.

When he'd gone, Frankie said, "Fliss, I don't mean to be funny, but what's happened to Andy's hair?"

Fliss giggled. "Mum made him put loads of Brylcreem in it and comb it into a quiff," she said.

The rest of us looked at each other in puzzlement, then we suddenly cottoned on. "It's very Fifties!" we chorused, and then all fell about laughing.

First off, we watched the film, and it was absolutely, fantastically brilliant. Sandy (the main girl in the film) and her friends even had a sleepover!

We bopped away to all the songs. Fliss knew most of them off by heart. Sometimes her mum couldn't resist coming in and bopping too – you could tell the theme for the sleepover had been her idea!

During the film we'd gorged ourselves on popcorn and Andy's yummy milkshakes. When it was finished, it was time for hot dogs and hamburgers with loads of mustard and ketchup, which Callum, Fliss's little brother, managed to smear all down his front. Then it was ice cream, with a choice of chocolate or strawberry sauce out of squeezy bottles. We were all in food heaven, though afterwards we felt so full we had to lie down on the sitting-room floor and have a *Grease* singalong while our tummies recovered.

After that Fliss's mum ordered Callum to bed and the five of us went up to Fliss's bedroom.

"You know what was great as well in that film?" said Lyndz, sitting down on the spare bed, which Fliss keeps covered with neat rows of about five hundred and one cuddly toys. "The dancing! That jive competition was cool! Couldn't we put some of the moves in our routine?"

"Great idea!" exclaimed Frankie. "Hey – we should have a go now while we remember!"

Apprehensively I glanced at Fliss. Up until now, no one had mentioned the dance competition. I figured it was still a sore subject.

But the next minute, Kenny said, "Fliss! You know the film really well. Can you show us some moves?" And straight away Fliss's expression changed from about-to-turn-grumpy to really keen. *Smart move, Kenny!* I thought, feeling relieved.

"Well, for a start there's hand-jive," Fliss said, "which means things like this." And she waggled her hands in front of her, holding each elbow in turn, and then doing something which looked like she was playing 'One potato, two potato' with herself.

We all had a go, and after a few false starts even I got some hand-jive moves going pretty well.

Kenny said, "What about those amazing

jumps, when the girl's legs swing right up?"

Some of the dancing in the film had been pretty acrobatic, with the boys flinging the girls around as if they were rag dolls.

"Oh, it's *seriously* tricky, that stuff," said Fliss.

"Let's have a go!" said Kenny. "That's *exactly* the sort of thing we should have in our routine. Gobsmackingly brilliant moves that'll leave the M&Ms gasping!" Fliss was hesitating, so Kenny held out her hands. "Come on!" she coaxed. "Can't be much harder than a piggyback, can it? I'm pretty strong, and you weigh about as much as one baked bean."

Which to Fliss – who worries about her weight because she's dead slim and *bananas* – was a big compliment. "OK, then," she said. She faced Kenny and put her hands on Kenny's shoulders. "Hold me round the waist," she said. "I'm going to do one little bounce, and then jump up with my legs either side of you, right? If you sort of bend forward into it, you can swing me back up into the air before I land."

Kenny nodded confidently, but I had a sneaking suspicion she didn't have a clue what Fliss was talking about.

"You sure about this?" Fliss asked. Kenny nodded again.

So Fliss did one little bounce on the spot, then she flung herself towards Kenny as if she were trying to hug her with her legs. Holding Fliss round the waist, Kenny swung forward like she'd been told to, till Fliss's feet were pointing to the ceiling.

"Er, I'm stuck," said Kenny in a strangulated voice.

Fliss was giggling. Her head was nearly on the floor. "Just swing me up again!" she said.

"Heeeeaaaaave!" groaned Kenny, putting all her strength into the swing.

She so nearly made it. She pulled Fliss upright again, although she didn't manage to swing her into the air, as Fliss had suggested. It would have been fine – if only Fliss's left foot, heading back towards the floor, hadn't got tangled in a loop of lace from her petticoats.

As she landed, Fliss stumbled, and since her arms were still round Kenny's neck, she pulled Kenny forward on top of her.

"Aaarrrgghh!"

They landed in a sprawled heap, and for a second Kenny just lay there, shaking with laughter.

"Get up," said Fliss.

"Hold your horses, I'm not that heavy," said Kenny.

"Get up!" Fliss screamed. "Get up, get up, *get up*!!!"

Quick as a flash, Kenny scrambled to her feet. "Fliss, are you OK?" she said.

By this time Frankie, Lyndz and I were clustered round her.

"No!" Fliss said, starting to sob. "It's my ankle. It..." She gasped as she tried to move. "It *really* hurts."

Together, the four of us managed to pull Fliss up. Her left leg had twisted at a really odd angle under her as she fell. Now Frankie supported her as she hopped to her bed and then half sat, half lay on it, propped up on her pillows.

"Does it still hurt?" asked Lyndz.

Fliss nodded, biting her lip. "*So* much."

"We'd better call her mum," I said to Frankie. But Fliss said, "No – no. It'll be OK in a minute. I'll just lie still for a bit."

"Let's think," said Kenny, a determined look on her face. "In football matches, when someone twists their ankle, they put an ice pack on it. D'you have an ice pack, Fliss?"

"I don't think so," said Fliss in a small voice. Her ankle obviously hurt – a *lot*.

"Won't a bag of frozen peas do?" said Frankie.

"Good thinking!" exclaimed Kenny. "I'll see if I can get to the freezer without anyone seeing me."

"The freezer's in the laundry room," said Fliss with a sob through gritted teeth. "Last door on the right before the kitchen."

"OK." Kenny opened Fliss's bedroom door a crack and looked both ways along the landing. "Coast clear," she mouthed, and tiptoed out.

By the time Kenny got back, holding the bag

of peas with her sleeves pulled down over her hands, Fliss was sniffing and pointing at her ankle in alarm. "It's gone all puffy!"

"Here, this'll stop the swelling," said Kenny, applying the peas.

Fliss winced at the cold. After a moment she wailed, "But I don't want a fat ankle!" For the first time since the accident, Kenny laughed.

It's strange, but sometimes when you've had a shock it can make you go giggly afterwards. Soon Kenny was re-enacting what had happened, with lots of exaggerated grimacing, and the rest of us were in hysterics. Even Fliss.

"How does it – hic – feel now?" hiccupped Lyndz.

"Oh, miles better," said Fliss breezily. She swung her legs off the bed. But the second she tried to stand on her left foot, she fell back again, her face twisted with pain.

"Aaaaaaah!"

"That's it," said Frankie. "Fliss. I'm telling your mum right now."

"OK," said Fliss in a trembly voice.

It was pandemonium. Fliss's mum thundered up the stairs and burst into the room like one of those doctors on *ER* racing into the operating theatre.

"My baby! Are you all right?" she screeched.

"Oh, Mummy!" wailed Fliss, suddenly far more upset than she'd been before.

"Tell me exactly what happened," said Mrs Sidebotham, taking Fliss's hand and smoothing her hair back, over and over.

While Fliss went through it all in minute detail, Andy shouted up the stairs, "Is everything OK?" about every three seconds. Not surprisingly, the hubbub woke Callum, who came out on to the landing, trailing his blanket and making small grizzling noises. His grizzling got louder when he realised no one was taking the least bit of notice.

"Are you *sure* you can't stand on it?" Fliss's mum asked her. Fliss tried again, and yelped with pain.

"OK," said Mrs Sidebotham, "we'll have to get you to the hospital."

"Oh, please," said Kenny, "may I come too? I want to be a doctor, you see—"

"No, Laura, I think it's best not," said Fliss's mum firmly. She already looked totally stressed. Having Kenny for company would probably have pushed her over the edge.

She looked round at the rest of us, and for one awful moment I thought she was going to burst into tears. But instead she said, "Rosie, Lyndsey – would you go and ask Andy to come up here? Felicity will need carrying down to the car."

"Yes, Mrs Sidebotham," said Lyndz and I together, and we raced downstairs.

We told Andy what had happened to Fliss and he dashed up the stairs. A minute later he came down again, much slower this time, carrying Fliss like she was some injured heroine in a film. Mrs Sidebotham opened the front door for them and then we heard the car doors slamming and the engine starting up.

When Andy came back he gave us a wobbly smile and said, "Don't worry about Fliss, girls. You go back up to your friends."

So Lyndz and I slunk back upstairs to Fliss's bedroom. There we found Kenny and Frankie sitting on Fliss's bed, and looking as cheerful as two wet weekends.

"What happens now?" I asked.

Frankie shrugged. "We wait, I guess. Fliss's mum said it was too late to ring any of our parents. So the sleepover's still on." She smiled weakly.

"How long d'you think Fliss'll be at the hospital?" asked Lyndz.

"It could take a while," said Kenny. "Sometimes there are loads of people in Casualty, and you just have to wait your turn."

If it hadn't been so awful it would have been funny, imagining Fliss and her mum waiting in Casualty in matching Fifties outfits, with matching ankle socks and matching blonde ponytails.

But none of us felt much like giggling any more. "Come on," I said, "we may as well get ready for bed." So we brushed our teeth and changed into our pyjamas, then wriggled inside our sleeping bags. Kenny put out the main light and we all switched on our torches.

"I bet Fliss'll come back and it'll turn out she's fine," said Lyndz. "Remember that time at Mrs McAllister's stables, when Fliss was riding Alfie and he suddenly shot off at a million miles an hour?"

"That was scary!" said Frankie. "If she'd fallen off she could have been so badly injured!"

"Exactly," said Lyndz. "But it turned out she was OK. It'll be the same tonight, you'll see."

"She might just be badly bruised," I said, nodding. But I was only pretending to share Lyndz's optimism. In my tummy I had a cold, sick feeling of dread.

"Rosie! Wake up!"

I heard Lyndz's voice and felt her nudging me in the ribs.

"Wha...?" I mumbled sleepily. "What time is it?"

"Half past one," said Frankie. "Fliss is back."

In a second I was awake. I scrambled out of my sleeping bag and shot to the window, where the others were craning their necks to see the car in the drive below.

"Is she all right? Can you see?" I said anxiously.

"She's getting out..." said Kenny. "She's OK. She's – Ohmigosh!"

"What?" There was a pause. "Kenny?"

"She's on crutches," said Kenny flatly. "Her leg's in plaster."

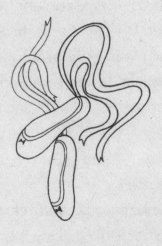

8

Lyndz had been wrong. Totally wrong. Fliss wasn't fine. She had broken her ankle.

"Well, two of the little bones in it, anyway," Fliss explained when she joined us in the bedroom.

Now she was sitting on the bed, still in her *Grease* outfit, her crutches propped against the wall. Her left leg was stuck out in front of her with what looked like a big red boot on it, except that her bare toes were poking out of the end.

"Can I touch it?" I asked, stretching my fingers gingerly towards the cast.

"Go ahead," said Fliss. "It's totally set."

"How come the plaster's red?" asked Frankie.

"You can choose different colours," said Fliss. "It's a new thing. I wanted pink, really, but they said they didn't have it."

Fliss didn't look half as miserable as you might expect. It sounded like she'd quite enjoyed being made a fuss of at the hospital. "The doctor was *lovely*," she said, smiling dreamily.

To be honest, it was Kenny I felt most sorry for right then. She was trying to put a brave face on it, but I could tell she felt just awful.

"It was an accident," I said to her quietly, when she passed me on her way to the bathroom. "Don't blame yourself."

"Thanks, Rosie," she said. "I know you want to be nice, but don't pretend. It was my fault, and I know it."

The next morning, on the way home in the car, I told Mum what had happened.

"Poor Felicity," said Mum, shaking her head. "And poor Nikki, too." (Nikki is Fliss's mum.) "I can just imagine how stressed she must have been. If this had happened when you were all at our house..." Mum shuddered.

After a minute, we stopped at some traffic lights and she turned to me with a serious look. "Rosie," she said. "I hope you girls will realise now just how dangerous your messing about can be."

"Yes, Mum," I said.

"You have to try and see the consequences of things," she went on as the lights changed. "Try to *think*. I know you'd like me to treat you more as a grown-up sometimes, but this is exactly what being a grown-up is about..."

Blah, blah, blah. I expect you can imagine the rest, so I won't bore you with it. Mum's lovely, but she doesn't half go on sometimes, especially when something worries her. We got all the way home before the lecture finished, and by then I'd said "Yes, Mum" about ninety times. Yawn!

That afternoon, I had a phone call from Frankie. "I've had an ace idea," she said, "for cheering Fliss up."

"Spill," I said.

"Tomorrow, we all take to school loads of stickers and glitter and coloured pens and stuff, and at break we can decorate her cast, and make it look really cool."

"Excellent!" I said. "I'm not sure whether I've got any stickers, though. It's a shame it's Sunday or I could go and buy some."

"Just bring whatever you've got," said Frankie.

So I spent the rest of the afternoon turning my bedroom upside down, looking for anything sparkly or spangly that might help jazz up Fliss's plaster cast. I did find some stickers – some really beautiful cat ones that I'd been given for my last birthday. I hesitated over them, because I'd been saving them up for something really special. To be honest with you, I didn't want to part with them. Who would know, after all, if I just told the others I hadn't got any stickers? But then I felt mean, and I put them in my school bag along with my glitter-glue pens and some sequins I'd found in my sewing box.

On Monday morning Fliss caused a big stir, hobbling into school on crutches. As she made her way through the playground half our class trailed after her, most of them wanting to have a go on her crutches.

"She's loving it!" Frankie whispered to me. And it was true. Fliss was basking in the attention, a big smile on her face.

"I know why, too," I said, nudging Frankie and pointing to one of the people clustered round Fliss. "Suddenly Ryan Scott's interested!"

At break time, Frankie, Kenny, Lyndz and I persuaded Fliss to park herself on a bench while we went to work on her cast with all our decorations.

"It's so sweet of you guys!" she giggled.

"It's the least we could do, Fliss," said Kenny earnestly. "Here, look – I've brought you something to keep your toes warm." She held up a large sock with a picture of a birthday cake on it. "When you press like this..." she said, jabbing at the cherry on top of the cake, "... it plays 'Happy Birthday'!"

The buzzy little sound, coming from something as ridiculous as a sock, made us all crack up. "It's awful!" said Fliss. "Brilliantly awful! Where did you get it?"

"It's my dad's," said Kenny. "But don't worry," she added, when she saw Fliss's nose wrinkling, "he's never worn it."

What with the sock, the stickers, the glitter, and all the swirls Kenny drew with her silver and gold pens, Fliss's cast ended up looking like a mad miniature Christmas tree.

"Is your mum cross about the accident?" Kenny asked, when at last we sat back to admire our handiwork.

"Not cross," said Fliss. "More disappointed, I think, because we've had to cancel the skiing holiday."

"What – *no one's* going?" asked Lyndz.

"Well, they were hardly going to leave me behind, were they?" said Fliss indignantly. "And they couldn't take me. I would have died of boredom sitting in the hotel all day while Mum and Andy were off skiing."

I saw Kenny's shoulders slump. At that moment I think we all felt bad, realising that we'd ruined a holiday for Fliss's entire family.

"Hey!" said Frankie suddenly. "Now you can come to the party on the last day of term!"

Fliss smiled ruefully. "Mmm. But I can't dance with the rest of you, can I?"

There was a moment's silence. Then Lyndz said, "Why don't you take charge of the costumes, Fliss? We so need your advice."

Fliss nodded. "OK," she said. "I guess I shouldn't let *all* my talents go to waste."

There was less than two weeks to go now, before the party. We began spending every break time rehearsing in the only private spot we could think of – that's right, by those pongy bins – with Fliss acting as look-out in case the M&Ms or any other spies from our class came along.

It was weird having a whole section missing from the routine – the bit when Fliss had come to the front to do her solo. We filled the gap by repeating the chorus steps, but they didn't go quite as well with that bit of the music.

"It's not the same without you, Fliss," said Kenny.

"Of course it isn't," said Fliss briskly. "But you'll just have to manage somehow, won't you?"

On Thursday each of us brought in a selection of clothes that we thought might be suitable. Fliss laid them out on one of the benches in the girls' changing room, so that she could see them all together.

"You should be in *toning* colours," she said strictly, hobbling up and down, and removing items she disapproved of. "I'm thinking pinks and purples, with quite a bit of silver." (Which is Frankie's favourite colour – all the silver things were hers.)

Kenny – who is definitely *not* a pinks and purples kind of person – was chewing her lip in a desperate attempt to stop herself saying "Yeuch!" She only just succeeded.

Fliss handed garments to each of us, and told us to stand in a line, holding them up. I had a purple T-shirt (my own) and a short pink skirt (Fliss's). I wasn't at all sure the skirt would fit me.

Suddenly we heard the growly voice of Emily Berryman behind us. "Working out costumes, are you?" she said. Then she added, really sarcastically, "Mmm. *Lovely.*"

Emma Hughes was standing beside her. "It's touching, really," she said to Emily, in a loud voice so that we could hear. "They haven't a clue how hopeless they're going to look next to us, have they?"

And with that, they went cackling off down the corridor like two horrid witches.

"Losers!" shouted Kenny after them. Which

was exactly what we hoped they were going to be next week.

I was worried, though. With Fliss's section missing from our routine, it just wasn't the same. The whole thing felt unbalanced, somehow.

Though I wasn't really aware of it, I must have kept turning the problem over and over in some dark corner of my brain, because on Tuesday, three days before the competition, I suddenly felt like a light bulb had been switched on inside my head.

It was slap bang in the middle of a maths lesson, and we were having my least favourite thing in the whole world: a mental arithmetic test. I was so amazed by this thing that had come zinging into my brain, that I didn't even hear three of the questions Mrs Weaver read out, and I didn't write any answers for three more.

As soon as the bell rang at the end of the lesson, I dashed between the desks, dodging shoving bodies. "Fliss, Fliss," I said breathlessly. "You *shall* go to the ball!"

Fliss turned round. She'd just levered herself up on her crutches. "What on earth are you talking about, Rosie?"

I was so excited I must have looked mad. "The party," I said. "I've just had the most wonderful idea!"

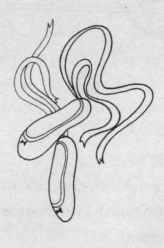

"Hand-jive???"

We were out in the playground. Fliss, Frankie, Kenny and Lyndz were looking at me in amazement.

"Of course!" I said. "Don't you see? It's perfect! Fliss can't join in with the whole routine, obviously, but when it's her turn to do a solo, she can come to the front and do a wicked hand-jive. She won't have to move her feet at all."

Suddenly Frankie cracked a big grin. "Rosie," she said. "You're a genius. It is perfect!"

"But what about my crutches?" asked Fliss. "I need them to get into position, but while I'm doing the hand-jive I won't be able to hold them."

"That's easy," I said. "Once you've got to the front, two of us can step forward and take the crutches. We can give them back to you at the end of your spot."

"Can you make up a routine in time for Friday?" Kenny asked Fliss.

"Thursday," corrected Lyndz. "Mrs Weaver said she wants to have a look at the routines the afternoon before the competition, remember?"

"Of course I can!" said Fliss. "What's a little hand-jive when I could have been Gwen Stefani?"

That set us all off laughing. "Way to go, Fliss!" giggled Lyndz.

"Hang on, there is one problem," said Fliss suddenly. "You're all sorted with costumes, but I don't have anything to wear."

"I'll give you mine," said Kenny quickly. She was just dying to get out of wearing the pink shorts Fliss had chosen for her.

"No, wait," I said, "I've got another suggestion. Because you're missing your skiing holiday, Fliss – and because they'll fit our colour scheme, too – I reckon you should wear your pink salopets."

"Hey, yeah!" said Lyndz. "We're all dying to see them."

"Really?" Fliss looked pleased. "They'll be a bit warm, but I guess I won't be moving around much – and I can change out of them after our routine. OK, Rosie, you're on!"

This was how the Sleepoverbabes were now complete. And how Fliss came to be dressed for our routine like a pink Abominable Snowman. I hadn't realised salopets were so all-over-thick-and-squashy. In their own strange way they were quite stylish, I suppose. They just looked a bit out of place in a Cuddington Primary classroom, rather than out on some glamorous Alpine mountainside.

Fliss wore them for the first time that Thursday in the lunch hour, when Mrs Weaver made each group go through their routine in our classroom.

"What's she want to see it for?" hissed Kenny, as we were waiting outside for our turn. "Is she worried we'll be singing rude words, or taking our clothes off, or something?"

"Maybe she's *hoping* that's what we'll do," snorted Frankie.

"Hey, take a look at this!" said Lyndz. She was standing on tiptoe, peering through the glass in the classroom door. "It's the M&Ms and Alana!"

Quick as a flash, we squashed up like sardines against the door, so we could all get a peek.

"What's the Queen doing?" said Kenny. "She's moving really jerkily."

"She's standing on her toes!" gasped Frankie. "Look! Right on the ends like a ballerina!"

It was true. Emma Hughes was wearing pink ballet shoes with ribbons criss-crossed round her ankles. And she was standing on the ends of them.

"She doesn't seem very comfortable," I said. "She looks like she's walking on stilts."

"And check out her face," laughed Kenny. "It's like she's sucking a lemon!"

"Who cares whether she's comfy or not? This is disastrous!" wailed Fliss. "They're doing ballet, aren't they? And Emma's doing proper pointe work! Didn't I tell you that that's what Lorna and Sean would go for? They're bound to win!"

"It's not good," agreed Lyndz. "Not good at all. Rosie, that's what their secret weapon must've been – those ballet shoes."

"I guess," I said gloomily.

"Well, there's nothing we can do about it now," said Frankie. "And it's a good job we didn't decide on a ballet routine ourselves. We would've been relying on you, Fliss, so we would've been in a right fix now."

"We'll just have to stick to our routine," said Kenny.

When the M&Ms had finished, Lyndz opened the door and we went into the classroom. We heard Mrs Weaver saying, "Emma, are you really sure you know how to dance in those shoes?"

"Oh *yes*, Mrs Weaver," Emma replied, with a smug glance in our direction. "I go to lessons, you know."

It was a useful trial run, doing the routine in front of Mrs Weaver. It went quite well, though I bumped into Kenny at one point, which made her forget the steps. Mrs Weaver thought Fliss was brave to be taking part.

"And I like the hand-jive, Felicity," she said. "It's very catchy!" As she said this she tried to copy some of the movements, but she got them hopelessly wrong. I didn't dare look at the others. I knew if I made eye contact with any of them I'd burst out laughing.

"Were we fantastic or what?" said Frankie in the changing room afterwards. "Weaver loved it! We just need to do the same tomorrow and we'll *definitely* win."

117

"Tomorrow's the scary part," I said. The thought of dancing in front of Lorna and Sean made me really nervous. They were such cool dancers themselves, I couldn't imagine they'd do anything but laugh at us.

The next morning the whole school was buzzing with excitement about the party. First thing after Assembly, our class and Mr Pownall's class joined forces to decorate the hall. Mr Pownall and Mrs Weaver climbed great big step-ladders and strung banners from the ceiling which said:

They hung up the lanterns we'd made in Art, too, while we covered every inch of wall space we could reach with the paintings and collages people had made.

"Those lanterns look so excellent from a distance!" said Frankie. "You'd never guess they're made of sweet wrappers and tin foil."

Meanwhile, other classes were helping set up trestle tables round the edges of the room and covering them with big tablecloths. Plates of yummy things like flapjacks, fairy cakes, chocolate brownies and muffins were starting to appear.

"Oooh, what a shame they're all covered in clingfilm," said Lyndz, who was practically drooling even though it wasn't long past breakfast time. "I'd love to sneak a taste."

I nodded. But to tell you the truth, I couldn't have eaten a thing, even if you'd wafted the gooiest chocolate cake in the world under my nose. My stomach felt like it was trying to tie knots in itself, and my teeth were chattering, though I had my cardie on and I wasn't cold.

"What time's the competition?" I said to Kenny.

"Eleven," she replied, breaking off a piece of Sellotape with her teeth. "You asked me that five minutes ago!"

"I think I'll go to the loo again," I said. That was the other effect nerves were having on me!

At eleven o'clock our whole class was sitting cross-legged in the hall (except for Fliss, of course, who was on a chair with her Christmas-tree leg stuck out in front of her). There were so many different sorts of costumes, it looked like we'd raided a fancy dress shop. Ryan Scott and three of his friends had gone for the RnB look, with low-slung baggy jeans, long-sleeved tops, and baseball caps. One group were all in dark glasses, and there was someone dressed up as Woody from *Toy Story* ("Weird!", as Frankie said). The M&Ms and Alana had leotards on, and wafty chiffon skirts, which I spotted Fliss eyeing enviously.

But, don't worry: no one outdid the Sleepoverbabes. As well as my purple T-shirt and pink skirt, I had a silver belt round my waist, and tiny silver butterfly clips in my hair. Kenny looked great in the pink shorts, even though she didn't like them, and somehow she'd persuaded Molly to lend her a white T-shirt with 'Kylie' written in silver across the front. Kenny thought it was the most ridiculous thing ever – "But I love the way Fliss *really* thinks it's cool!" she whispered to me.

Frankie, to everyone's amazement, had dug out a silver jumpsuit at the last minute, and she'd been striding around like a space action hero. (She's got some seriously mad things lurking in the back of her wardrobe!) Fliss was in her salopets, of course, and Lyndz looked ace in a lilac crop top and deep purple mini skirt. We were all wearing trainers and I'd bought some silver laces for mine, specially.

But the finishing touch was the best. Fliss had brought in some silver body glitter – it's like moisturiser with sparkly bits in – and we'd all rubbed that on our cheeks and arms, so they shimmered when we moved. In short, we looked mega, MEGA fantastic.

When Mrs Weaver led Lorna and Sean into the hall, everyone went quiet.

"Hi again," said Sean, with a friendly grin. "It's good to be back!"

"We're really looking forward to seeing your dances," added Lorna.

At which my tummy groaned, and I had to clutch it to make it shut up.

Lorna and Sean sat down, while Mrs Weaver went over to the tape player. She had everyone's tapes lined up, and was going to call us in turn.

First up were the group in the shades. Then it was Alana and the M&Ms.

They got into position, and Emily Berryman nodded to Mrs Weaver to start the tape. Soon Emma Hughes was tottering around on the tips of her toes.

A second later, Lorna sprang out of her

chair, shouting "Stop!" Mrs Weaver leapt at the tape machine and the music clunked off. Emily and Alana stumbled to a halt. Emma Hughes looked really cross at having been interrupted.

"Where did you get those shoes, Emma?" asked Lorna, sounding quite agitated. "They're not yours, are they?"

"They are!" said Emma. Now she was beginning to look nervous. "I found them in a jumble sale."

"*A jumble sale?*"

"What's wrong with jumble sales?" Kenny whispered to me.

Lorna said, "Pointe shoes must be carefully fitted. You can't just wear any old pair. And you need years of training before you can dance on your toes."

Emma's chin had started to tremble. "I-I'm sorry..." she stammered. "I thought—"

"Oh, Emma!" interrupted Mrs Weaver crossly. "You told me you went to ballet lessons!"

"I do!" said Emma.

"But you don't wear pointe shoes for your lessons, do you?" said Lorna.

Miserably, Emma shook her head.

"I'm sorry to seem harsh," said Lorna, coming forward and putting a hand on Emma's shoulder, "but this is very important. I can see you're nowhere near strong enough to start pointe work. And if you dance on your toes without the right training it can do terrible damage to your feet. So don't do it, OK?"

"OK," mumbled Emma.

"Now, do you want to take the shoes off and start again without them?" Lorna suggested.

I could see that that was the very last thing Emma wanted to do, but she didn't have much choice.

"So much for secret weapons!" I whispered to Lyndz, who nodded and grinned.

"Serves her right for being so smug," she whispered back. "Though I feel a bit sorry for her too. It's dead embarrassing!"

Without the novelty of Emma dancing on

the tips of her toes, the M&Ms' dance was really boring. Well before the end, everyone was shuffling and fidgeting, obviously wishing it was over.

"Thanks very much, girls," said Lorna when at last the music came to an end. "That was lovely." But I could tell she was only being polite.

What a disaster for the M&Ms! They sat down with majorly crabby looks on their faces. Like Lyndz, I was almost beginning to feel sorry for them, but then Mrs Weaver said, "Felicity! Your group next," so we grabbed our headsets, scrambled to our feet, and all at once we were on!

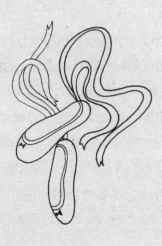

10

Step, kick, shoulder, shoulder – hands up, turn around...

As the familiar music blared, I concentrated as hard as I possibly could. Just getting my hands and feet working in the right order felt as complicated as conducting a whole orchestra!

And – miracle of miracles – I made it through the first half of the routine without a mistake. But when I moved to the front for my solo, it was as if someone had suddenly pressed the

'Erase' button in my head – I went completely blank! For one dreadful, goose-pimply moment I thought I was just going to stand there like a lemon. But then I found myself repeating two of the steps from the chorus section, over and over. OK, it wasn't the most exciting solo in the world but, boy, was I relieved! I felt like a goalie in a football match who'd just made a really tricky save.

Fliss's solo went down a storm, and no one else forgot a thing. At the end there was a big round of applause.

"Were we hot, or what?" panted Frankie, as we went to sit down again.

I was hot all right – but maybe not in the way Frankie meant!

Now that my nerves had totally disappeared I really enjoyed watching the other groups. When it came to the end I'd even forgotten about the competition bit, and that Lorna and Sean were going to pick a winner.

It was only when they left the hall for a few

minutes to talk about it in private that I started getting excited.

"All hold hands!" commanded Frankie. I grabbed Lyndz on one side of me, and reached up to Fliss on the other.

As Lorna and Sean came back into the hall, Frankie sent hand-squeezes back and forth along our line like a Mexican wave. I held my breath. I realised that, even though it'd made me so nervous, I really wanted to win, so we'd have another chance to do our routine.

"You all did brilliantly," said Sean. "Why did you have to make our lives so difficult by being so good? We nearly came to blows out there trying to choose a winner!"

Everyone laughed.

"And, in fact," Sean went on, "we're going to cheat a bit, because we've decided we'd like two groups to perform at the party tonight. A winner and a runner-up, if you like."

"So, let's get on with the announcements," said Lorna. "The winner is... the RnB group.

That's Ryan and company, isn't it? Well done, guys, it was a brilliant routine!"

I dropped Lyndz and Fliss's hands to clap along with everyone else. My heart had sunk into my trainers. It made me feel mean, because Ryan and his mates had been really good.

"But that's not all," said Sean, "because we simply couldn't let the party miss out on a bit of hand-jive..."

Hand-jive? I thought dimly. Who did hand-jive apart from us?

"So," Sean was saying, "Sleepoverbabes – will you strut your stuff for us tonight as well?"

"Yeaaaah!" Frankie punched the air.

"Super-coo-el!" Kenny shouted.

"And I think you should teach everyone the moves," said Lorna. "You'll be a big hit!"

And you know what? Lorna was right. We were the biggest hit, I reckon, in the history of Cuddington Primary.

The party was totally fab. The school hall looked amazing. The caretaker, as well as building the stage at one side of the hall, had rigged up coloured lights and an enormous mirror ball which spun round as the music played, reflecting flashes of orange and green and red over what ended up being a scrum of dancing bodies.

Hang on, though – I'm getting ahead of myself, cos to start with no one danced much at all. There were loads of people there: pupils and teachers, mums and dads, kid brothers and sisters, grans and grandpas – all ages from the babies to the wrinklies.

"Wow, lots of people have dressed up," Lyndz said as the hall started filling up, with everyone congregating round the food and drink tables.

"Yeah, and some of them look really cool," added Frankie. Then she dug me in the ribs and nodded towards the door. I spun round – just in time to see the M&Ms stalking into the room wearing nasty matching crop tops and gross stripey leggings. Frankie and I looked at each other. "Not!" we said together, and burst out laughing.

Frankie, Lyndz, Kenny, Fliss and I were in our Sleepoverbabes gear, of course, and looking so ace it was all we could do to stop ourselves admiring each other the whole time. But there was plenty of other stuff to grab our attention. For a start, we all had our families there. Mum and Adam had come, and I was really surprised that Tiff had tagged along too at the last minute.

"Though I don't know why I'm bothering, cos it's bound to be really naff," she'd said in the car.

"Take no notice, Rosie," Mum had said, winking at me.

"No fear!" I'd grinned. Even grouchy Tiff couldn't spoil this party, I knew that right from the start!

Nikki and Andy were there as well, and Nikki was looking amazing in a tight sequinny dress.

Everyone got a good look at it, too, because when the first raffle was drawn her ticket was the winner and she went up on stage to collect the prize.

"Oooh, champagne! My favourite!" she cooed, as Sean handed her a great big bottle of the stuff and gave her a kiss on the cheek. Nikki went bright pink – just like Fliss does when we tease her about Ryan Scott – and everyone clapped and cheered.

After Nikki had come down from the stage I spotted Kenny stalking towards her, looking grim and determined. She talked to Nikki for quite a while, and Nikki put her arm round her and smiled a lot as she answered.

"What was all that about?" I said, catching hold of Kenny's elbow as she pushed her way back through the crush towards the crisps-and-sarnies table.

"I wanted to give Fliss's mum a kind of formal apology," said Kenny, looking mightily relieved. "For ruining their skiing holiday and stuff. She was really nice about it. You know what she said?"

"What?"

Kenny was grinning wickedly. "She said getting a bottle of champagne and a kiss from Sean made it all worthwhile – especially the kiss from Sean!"

Not long after that it was time for the dance routines. Lorna introduced Ryan's group first, explaining about the competition and how we'd all been so good they'd had to pick two groups as winners.

The RnB routine went down really well, though most people stood and watched rather than joining in the dancing.

"Us next, us next, us next," Lyndz kept muttering nervously as the five of us waited at the side of the stage for the routine to finish. She was squeezing my hand so tightly I thought I wasn't going to have a drop of blood left in it!

A second later Lorna was back on stage, calling on everyone to "... give a big, warm,

Cuddington Primary welcome to the Sleepoverbabes!" Lyndz seemed rooted to the spot with nerves, so I gave her a gentle shove in the back and followed her on to the stage.

If I didn't seem nervous myself it was a total act. I could happily have turned round and legged it right out of the hall. But it wasn't long before I found myself grinning so much my face hurt. There was I, Rosie Maria Cartwright, with my four best friends in the world, dancing on stage in front of a big cheering crowd. It felt totally awesome – like we were real pop stars. What could be better?

And the more I felt myself relax and enjoy it, the easier the steps became. It was like my arms and legs knew what to do all by themselves. I didn't make a single mistake. Spooky!

"Yo!" shrieked Kenny next to me, wiggling her shoulders, then whipping round in a slick turn.

We were having such a fab time up there it must have been infectious, because by the time we were half way through the routine everyone was bopping along. In amongst the crowd I could see Mum and Tiffany (who didn't seem to think the party was so naff after all) taking it in turns to spin Adam round in his wheelchair. It made him shriek as loud as Kenny.

At the end everyone started chanting "Encore! Encore!" louder and louder.

"Does that mean they want us to do it again?" I asked Kenny.

"Sure does!" Kenny laughed.

"*Before they start*..." yelled Lorna above the cheering, flapping her hands to get everyone to quieten down. "Before they start – how about Felicity teaches us her hand-jive moves? Then we can all join in!"

A big roar of "*Yeeeeaaaah*!!" went up from the crowd. Fliss looked chuffed, and nervous, and embarrassed – all at once.

She'd come up with a name for each move, so she shouted them out as she demonstrated.

"Mashed potato!" she yelled, hitting her fists one on top of the other.

"Mashed potato!" echoed a hallful of people, copying her.

"See ya later!" called Fliss, jerking her thumb over her shoulder.

Then – "Twizzle sticks!" – she rolled her hands round each other.

And – "Pancake flips!" – she shimmied her hands, flat, over and under each other.

It was a scream. Second time around, as Fliss's bit of the music came up she screamed, "Hand-jive! C'mon everybody!" and suddenly we were faced with the amazing sight of everyone in the hall doing our routine.

When our track came to an end Fliss's mum, who was down at the front right by the stage, put two fingers in her mouth and gave an enormous whooping whistle. I was gobsmacked – Fliss's mum usually tries to be so ladylike!

"Looks like she's having a good time, huh?" said Kenny, coming up behind me and sticking her chin on my shoulder.

"And then some!" I said.

We were so hot from the dancing that when we jumped down from the stage we made straight for the drinks table. And that was when I spotted you, and I just knew I had to race over straight away and tell you about all the mad things that've been happening!

Phew, we've been sitting here gassing for ages! D'you want to come and have a dance? We've been missing loads of great music. I dare you to dance near Kenny. Look at her – she's a hazard, that girl!

What's that? Fliss – where? Oh blimey, you're right. Lorna's signing her plaster cast. And look, there's Fliss's mum, talking to Sean again. Her face is a picture – totally starstruck!

Hey, you know what? I've just had a wicked idea. We should get Ryan Scott to sign Fliss's cast – don't you think? She'll blush as red as her plaster! Oh listen, that's Frankie, yelling for me. I bet you anything she's just had the same idea. I'd better go – but I'll catch you later!

Kenny's Top Ten Dance-off Dvds

Here are my must-see movies for any dance-off sleepover!

1. High School Musical 1 and 2
2. Hairspray
3. Grease 1 and 2
4. Strictly Ballroom
5. Singing in the Rain
6. Step Up
7. Fantasia
8. Mary Poppins
9. Honey
10. Any Hannah Montana DVD!

Kenny xx

Steal that Style with Fliss's Dance-off Makeover

Look fantastic at your dance-off sleepover with my Grease-inspired 50s look!

Wear a floaty, brightly coloured skirt (with lots of netting underneath to give it volume, if you have any).

Top this with a slim-fitting shirt, tucked in.

Add a wide belt or tie a ribbon around your waist.

Tie a silk scarf around your neck and knot it at the side.

Put long hair in a high ponytail or wear a bright headband if you have short hair.

Finish off your 50s look with some flat shoes and get dancing!

Fliss ✗

Rosie's Dance-off
Raspberry Milkshake

For cooling off after
all that dancing!
You will need:

- 110g (4oz) raspberries

- 300 ml chilled semi-skimmed milk

- 250 ml plain yoghurt

Place all the ingredients into a blender and
liquidise until smooth.
If you don't have raspberries, try strawberries
or bananas – and enjoy!

Rosie x

Bop to the top with your own dance-off competition!

 Choose your favourite music or a film to dance to.

 Design your own outfits – bring some dancing clothes and create your own pop or film-star look.

 Try a style of dancing you've not done before – ballet dancing, tap dancing, line dancing, ballroom dancing.

 Make up your own dance routines and get grooving!

That's all for now, guys. See you next time – for our brilliant beach party…

Rosie x

You are invited to join Frankie, Lyndz, Fliss, Rosie and me on our next crazy adventure in...

The Sleepover Club

Hit the Beach!

I L.O.V.E. sports and am soooo excited about our school trip. A week away from home with my best friends by the seaside - time to catch some waves!

Are **you** up for some fun in the sun? Grab your shades and join the club!

From

Kenny x